Vegetarian
Four Seasons

Rose Elliot is the bestselling author of several vegetarian cookery books. A vegetarian since the age of three, she has never eaten meat, but loves the scope which vegetarian cookery gives for imagination and creativity. She contributes to the national press, is in great demand as a cookery demonstrator and broadcasts on radio and television.

Vegetarian Four Seasons

A Cook's Calendar of Delicious Recipes

ROSE ELLIOT

Thorsons
An Imprint of HarperCollinsPublishers

Thorsons
An Imprint of HarperCollins*Publishers*
77–85 Fulham Palace Road,
Hammersmith, London W6 8JB

First published by HarperCollins*Publishers* 1993
Thorsons edition 1996
1   3   5   7   9   10   8   6   4   2

© Rose Elliot 1993

Rose Elliot asserts the moral right to
be identified as the author of this work

A catalogue record for this book
is available from the British Library

ISBN 0 7225 3361 6

Printed and bound in Great Britain by
Caledonian International Book Manufacturing Ltd, Glasgow

Typeset by
Harper Phototypesetters Ltd, Northampton

CONTENTS

&

ACKNOWLEDGEMENTS

&

Working on this book has been a particularly happy experience, and I'd like to express my warmest thanks to everyone who has been involved. To Robin Wood, for inviting me to write the book in the first place, and to Polly Powell, for enthusiastically taking it up; to Barbara Dixon for her hard work on the manuscript, and to Caroline Hill, the art editor, and Joan Curtis, the designer, for making it look so good. Special thanks to my wonderful editor, Isabel Moore, and home economist Lyn Rutherford – both were a delight to work with, as always, and contributed many ideas. And not forgetting those whose support, help and understanding means so much to me: my husband, Robert, my daughters, and my agent, Barbara Levy.

INTRODUCTION

❧

As I worked on this book I realised more and more how much the seasons still affect us, even though, thanks to modern transportation and refrigeration, our cooking and eating are no longer tied to them in the way they once were. And I realised too how much the foods which are naturally available at a given time of year are in tune with the demands of that season and harmonise with our needs.

In winter, for instance, just when we feel like eating warming, substantial foods to keep out the cold, we have a wonderful range of root vegetables, designed by nature to be suitable for storing for many weeks. As spring approaches cleansing, astringent foods like fresh green leafy vegetables come into season, preparing us for the lighter meals and greater physical activity which comes with the return of the longer, warmer days. Then juicy fruits and vegetables refresh us in the warmth of summer. In autumn the seasonal produce becomes more substantial and filling as we move towards winter once again.

I've discovered how much pleasure and satisfaction there is in using seasonal produce and how it is often associated with traditional festivals and celebrations throughout the year, making these more special and enjoyable. Carl Jung said that fully experiencing every chapter of our lives, from childhood to old age, is vital for our complete well-being. In a similar way I think the same can be said of the seasons, each of which has its particular pleasures and qualities as well as its challenges. Being attuned to each season means accepting that, as in the whole of life, nothing is permanent. We have to enjoy what we have now, then let go, move on and enjoy the next moment.

So, there are a number of good reasons for using foods in season, and it can certainly make sense from an economic point of view. But, having said that, I would not like to think that anyone will feel they have to use this book rigidly. Do by all means enjoy out-of-season recipes if they take your fancy or you fall for something unseasonable but enticing in the supermarket – this kind of inspiration is all part of the pleasure of cooking. Happy cooking and eating.

Rose Elliot

SPRING

&

SPRING

ℛ

During spring the days get longer, the sun climbs higher in the sky each day, the sap rises and there's a feeling of new life and energy everywhere. Where I live, although spring does not officially begin until March we see the first promises in February, as the early crocuses and snowdrops push their way up through the hard earth and the early cherry delights us with its pink blossom – a resurgence of life that culminates in the celebration of Easter, with its focus on re-birth and resurrection. I love this time of year; the buds on the trees are bursting into leaf and the air is heady with blossom – so much external activity, yet underlying it there is a great stillness.

Spring is a time of transition. We are aware of this in the kitchen in the early spring as we use up the last of the stored fruits and vegetables and prepare for the arrival of the first of the new ones. The weather, too, at least where I live, is often unsettled. So spring cookery demands flexibility; a readiness to produce meals which protect us from the still-chilly winds and rainy days, or allow us to make the most of warm days with al fresco eating, picnics and lunches in the garden. And also to introduce new flavours as the substantial foods of winter give way to the lighter, fresher ones of the new season, as the precious early crops arrive.

It's interesting that many of these are quite astringent and even slightly bitter – rhubarb, for instance, and vegetables such as turnips, radishes, spring onions and even tender young dandelion leaves and nettles – which used to be eaten to cleanse and tone the system, country lore with which modern herbalists would agree. Even the first herbs – mint, chives and rocket – are ones which seem made for waking up our tastebuds and getting us ready for the new flavours of the incoming season.

The new spring root vegetables – carrots, turnips, spring onions, potatoes – are light and juicy, needing very short cooking times, different in nature from their mature, stored counterparts which have nourished us so well during the cold winter months. Another early home-grown crop is broad beans, which perfectly bridge the gap between the dried pulses of winter and the light vegetables of summer. Apart from rhubarb, which although technically not a fruit is used as such, and is pleasant for a change, spring is a sparse time for fruit and one during which we can justifiably enjoy the occasional treat of exotic fruits such as pineapple, mango and kiwi.

Spring is a natural time for eggs, which can be enjoyed in a variety of sweet and savoury dishes such as Frittata with Baby Carrots and Spring Onions (page 22), Savoury Spinach Gâteau (page 24) and Hot Lemon Soufflé (page 30). From a moral point of view, although I do not wish to eat animals which have been killed, I do not object to eating eggs because in a natural environment, unless fertilized and then incubated, eggs would simply lie around until they rotted and were re-absorbed into the earth. So why not eat them? It goes without saying, though, that they should be truly free-range, from a reliable, salmonella-free source and eaten in moderation as part of an all-round balanced diet.

SPRING STARTERS

&

New Vegetables with Aioli

You need a blender or food processor for this quick version of aioli, although you can adapt the recipe for making it by hand if you use two egg yolks instead of a whole egg, and add the oil drop by drop, as you whisk the mixture. The amount of garlic is very much a question of taste and can be reduced – or increased. The vegetables, too, can of course be varied. They can be served raw or, as in this version, cooked just to take the rawness off, then served warm. Although most people serve this as a starter, and a very good one it makes, my favourite way of eating this dish is as a main course, with my fingers rather than a knife and fork. It would serve four as a main course.

FOR THE AIOLI
2–3 garlic cloves
1 egg
¼ tsp salt
¼ tsp mustard powder
2–3 grindings of black pepper
2 tsp wine vinegar
2 tsp lemon juice
200ml/7 fl oz light olive oil or
    grapeseed oil

FOR THE VEGETABLES
2 fennel
8 baby turnips
450g/1 lb baby carrots
1 small cauliflower or
    2–4 miniature ones
450g/1 lb baby courgettes

First make the aioli. Put the garlic in a food processor or blender and purée it as smoothly as you can, then add the egg, salt, mustard, pepper, vinegar and lemon juice. Blend for a minute at medium speed until the ingredients are well mixed, then turn the speed up to high and gradually add the oil, drop by drop, through the top of the goblet. When you have added about half the oil, you will hear the sound change to a 'glug-glug' noise and you can add the rest of the oil more quickly, in a thin stream. Taste the aioli and adjust the seasoning if necessary. If it seems a bit on the thick side, you can thin it by beating in a teaspoonful or two of boiling water.

Next, prepare the vegetables. If they are young and tender, they will only need trimming and washing. Remove any tough layers from the fennel, then cut each bulb down first into quarters then into eighths. Trim and scrub the turnips and carrots. Cut the cauliflower or miniature cauliflowers as necessary, to produce chunky pieces for dipping in the aioli; halve or quarter the courgettes to make long slim batons if they are thick; if they are really slender, leave them whole.

Cook the fennel for about 8 minutes in fast-boiling water; remove the fennel, rinse under the cold tap to cool it quickly, then put it into a colander to drain thoroughly. Boil the turnips in the same water; as soon as they are just tender, drain and refresh them and put them in the colander with the fennel; repeat the process with the carrots and then the cauliflower. The vegetables will only take a minute or two to cook; keep testing them with the point of a knife, and remove them from the water as soon as they are just tender. Finally, cook the courgettes which will only take about 60 seconds.

Put the aioli into a shallow bowl on a large platter. Arrange the vegetables around it, patting them dry on kitchen paper as necessary before serving. (Serves 6–8)

For a vegan version of aioli, use the special mayonnaise recipe on page 44, using soya milk instead of single cream and 2–3 garlic cloves.

Japanese-Style Salad with Dipping Sauce and Gomasi

This is a light, refreshing first course. If you can't get rice vinegar, ordinary wine vinegar will do but it hasn't got quite the same sweetness and delicacy as rice vinegar (which you can get at some health shops or Chinese shops).

packet or bunch of radishes
bunch of spring onions
225g/8 oz mooli or turnip

FOR THE DIP
1 tbls grated fresh ginger

2 tbls soy sauce
2 tbls rice vinegar

FOR THE GOMASIO
4 tbls sesame seeds
2 tbls salt

Wash and trim all the vegetables. Cut the radishes into lotus flowers, if you are feeling enthusiastic, and pop them into a bowl of icy cold water for the petals to open. Cut the green part off each spring onion to leave about 5 cm/2 inch of the white part. Make cuts in the white part in from both ends towards the centre, then put them into the water, too, to curl. Peel the mooli or turnip and cut into thin sticks; make five equal cuts down each stick almost to the base and fold in the second and fourth sections to make a flower. All this can be done 2 hours or so before you want to serve the salad.

While the flowers are opening, make the dip by mixing together all the ingredients and then putting it into four tiny bowls, or one larger one if you prefer. Make the gomasio by putting the sesame seeds and salt into a dry frying pan set over a moderate heat. Stir for a couple of minutes or so as the sesame seeds toast and smell nutty and delicious, then remove from the heat. When the mixture has cooled, pulverize it in a coffee grinder, or with a pestle and mortar, or in a bowl, with the end of a wooden rolling pin. Put a small quantity into four tiny bowls, or one larger one.

Drain the flowers and arrange them on four plates. If you're using tiny bowls for the dip and gomasio, you might put these on the plates, too, as part of the arrangement, or serve them separately. (Serves 4)

Use a good quality soy sauce for the dipping sauce, one that's been naturally fermented, without the addition of caramel (read the label.)

Mediterranean Cooked Green Salad

The frequent, often daily, use of dark green leafy vegetables is one of the characteristics of the Mediterranean diet, and a typical and popular way of serving them is as a cooked salad, served warm or cold. Other ingredients, such as whole lentils or chopped hard-boiled eggs can be added, turning this simple dish into a complete light meal.

450g/1 lb spinach or other dark green leafy vegetables
4 spring onions
1 garlic clove, crushed (optional)
1–2 tbls lemon juice

2–3 tbls olive oil
salt and freshly ground black pepper
lemon wedges to garnish

Wash the spinach thoroughly. Put it into a dry saucepan, cover, and cook for 7–10 minutes, until it is tender, pressing down with a fish slice as it cooks. Drain the spinach in a colander, pressing out the water with the fish slice. Put into a bowl.

Wash, trim and chop the spring onions and add most of them to the spinach, saving some for a garnish. Mix the garlic with the lemon juice and olive oil and add to the spinach, stirring to make sure it is well distributed. Season with salt and pepper. Turn the mixture into a shallow dish and garnish with the remaining spring onions and some lemon slices. Serve warm or cold, with more olive oil for people to help themselves. (Serves 4)

Vegetable Terrine

This is a pretty starter – a loaf-shaped terrine of white curd cheese flecked with vegetable pieces of different colours, with a green coat of spinach and a vinaigrette sauce.

250g/9 oz spinach leaves
50g/2 oz French beans
50g/2 oz spring onions
50g/2 oz red pepper
olive oil
225g/8 oz curd cheese
2 tbls chopped fresh chives

2 eggs
salt and freshly ground black
   pepper

FOR THE VINAIGRETTE
2 tbls red wine vinegar
6 tbls olive oil

First set the oven to 160°C/325°F/Gas Mark 3, then line a 450 g/1lb loaf tin with a strip of non-stick paper to cover the base and extend up the narrow ends. The deep type of loaf tin is best if you have one.

Next, half-fill a fairly large saucepan with water and bring it to the boil. Meanwhile, wash the spinach; trim and wash the beans and spring onions; wash the red pepper and cut it into strips just less than 1 cm/½ inch wide. When the water boils, put it in the spinach and boil it for 1–2 minutes, until it is just soft, then drain it into a colander, saving the hot water, and refresh under the cold tap. Put the hot water drained from the spinach back into the pan, bring it to the boil, and put in the beans, spring onions and red pepper. Boil them for 2 minutes, then drain and refresh them under the cold tap. (You won't need the cooking water any more, but it now makes good stock.)

Brush the loaf tin with a little olive oil, then press a thin layer of spinach into the base and up the sides, so that they are all covered and there is enough spinach over to cover the top later. Pat the other vegetables dry on kitchen paper and cut them into 1 cm/½ inch lengths.

Put the curd cheese into a bowl with the chives and beat in the eggs, then add the pieces of vegetable and some salt and pepper to taste. Spoon the mixture into the spinach-lined tin and cover the top with the rest of the spinach. Stand the tin in a roasting tin and pour boiling water round it so that it comes half-way up the sides; bake for 1 hour. Let the terrine cool completely in the tin, then chill it.

Meanwhile, make the vinaigrette by putting the vinegar and oil into a small jar with some salt and pepper and shaking until combined. When you're ready to serve the terrine, cut it into slices about 1 cm/½ inch wide; put each slice on a plate and pour some vinaigrette beside it. (Serves 6–8)

Nettle Soup

In an age when you can buy strawberries in the middle of winter and leeks in midsummer, at least weeds are still seasonal, and this soup is a great way to celebrate the coming of spring!

1 tbls olive oil	salt and freshly ground black
1 onion, peeled and chopped	pepper
450g/1 lb tender nettles	grated nutmeg
150ml/5 fl oz single cream	

Heat the oil in a large saucepan, put in the onion and cook gently, covered, for 10 minutes.

Meanwhile, wash and roughly chop the nettles. Add them to the pan, along with 1.4 L/3 pints of water. Bring to the boil, then simmer for about 15 minutes, until the nettles are very tender. Whizz to a purée in a food processor and pour back into the pan through a sieve, pushing through as much of the nettles as you can.

Stir in the cream, adjust the consistency with a little more water if necessary to make a thin, light soup, then season with salt, pepper and freshly grated nutmeg. Serve in warmed bowls. (Serves 4)

For the nettle soup pick tender nettles from a pollution-free spot and wash them well before use.

Pink Grapefruit, Ruby Oranges and Mint

This pretty and refreshing mixture is good as a breakfast or brunch dish as well as a starter.

2 pink grapefruit   4 sprigs of fresh mint
4 ruby oranges

Holding a grapefruit over a bowl to catch the juice, cut off the skin and pith with a sharp knife, like peeling an apple when you want to make a long piece of peel; cut between the transparent membranes to release the juicy segments of fruit. Repeat the process with the other grapefruit and the oranges, which are a bit more fiddly to do. Add some fresh mint leaves to the mixture, and serve. (Serves 2–4)

Watercress Cream

Make this light and refreshing starter just before you want to serve it, so that the colour and flavour is fresh. Serve with some good bread.

packet or bunch of watercress   salt and freshly ground black
225g/8 oz fromage frais   pepper

Wash the watercress, removing any tough stems or damaged leaves. Reserve 4 good sprigs for garnishing; put the rest into a food processor with the fromage frais and whizz to a smooth purée, or chop the watercress finely by hand then stir it into the fromage frais. Either way, season with salt and freshly ground pepper. Divide the purée between four plates and garnish each with a sprig of watercress. (Serves 4)

Piquant Cucumber Salad

This is a refreshing starter, given a pleasant kick by the mustard seeds.

1 cucumber
2 tsp white mustard seeds
salt and freshly ground black
   pepper

3 tbls rice vinegar or white wine
   vinegar
fresh chives or young dill, if
   available

Peel the cucumber then cut it into quite thin slices. Layer these into a shallow dish, sprinkling the mustard seeds, some salt and a grinding of pepper between the layers. Pour the vinegar over the top. Cover the salad and leave for at least an hour, preferably longer – even overnight – for the flavours to blend. Snip over some fresh chives or dill before serving. (Serves 4–6)

Kohlrabi and Radish Salad

Kohlrabi has a delicate flavour which I find pleasant, but the thing which I like about it most is its very crisp yet tender, juicy texture. It makes it perfect for early spring salads.

3 tbls olive oil
1 tbls wine vinegar
salt and freshly ground black
   pepper

2 kohlrabi, about 225g/8 oz
   together
packet or bunch of radishes

Put the oil and vinegar into a bowl with salt and pepper to taste and mix to make a simple dressing. Peel the kohlrabi quite thinly, then cut it into julienne matchsticks; wash and slice the radishes. Add the kohlrabi and radishes to the bowl and stir gently to coat everything with the dressing. (Serves 4)

If you can't get kohlrabi, use turnip.

NEW VEGETABLES AND HERBS

§

Dandelion leaves make a delightful, slightly bitter addition to a green salad. Pick a small handful of leaves in a place free from pollution, and wash them well. Add them to a base of other salad greens – I find ordinary floppy lettuce a good neutral base for this kind of salad – tearing them up as you do so and dress with vinaigrette.

Little Broad Bean and Mint Patties

I like the crisp coating which chick-pea flour gives to these patties, although you could use ordinary flour, or even fry or bake them without flour, as they'll still get crisp. Some lightly seasoned yogurt is good with them, as well as a sauce made by stirring chopped chives into plain yogurt. Sliced tomatoes or a tomato salad, or Dandelion Leaf Salad also go well with them.

900g/2 lb shelled broad beans	salt and freshly ground black
2 tbls chick-pea flour plus extra	pepper
for coating	olive oil
6–8 sprigs of fresh mint	lemon slices

Cook the beans in boiling water for a few minutes until they are tender, then remove from the heat, drain, and leave until they are cool enough to handle. With your finger and thumb, pop the beans out of their grey jackets. Put the beans into a food processor with the 2 tablespoons of chick-pea flour, the mint and some salt and pepper, and whizz until a thick purée is formed. Divide this into eight portions, dip them in a little chick-pea flour and shape them into flat round patties.

Either shallow-fry the patties, turning them over so that they can get crisp and brown on both sides, or bake them in the oven. To do this, set the oven to 200°C/400°F/Gas Mark 6 and put a baking sheet in the oven to heat. Brush this with oil, then put the patties on it, turning them so that their tops are lightly coated with oil. Bake them for 12–15 minutes, turn them over and bake for about 10 minutes more to brown the other side. Serve the patties with lemon slices. (Serves 4)

Lemony Rice with Beans and Spring Onions

The lemon grass gives this dish a particularly good flavour but if you can't get it, some grated lemon rind does the job pretty well. The colours – primrose yellow rice and green vegetables – are very springlike. A watercress salad goes well with it, and some crunchy roasted cashew nuts or almonds, served from a small bowl so that people can help themselves. Any rice that's over makes a good salad, served cold.

225g/8 oz brown rice	3–4 lemon grass
1 tsp turmeric	225g/8 oz French beans
salt and freshly ground black pepper	4–6 spring onions
	2 tbls fresh lemon juice

Put the rice into a medium-large heavy-based saucepan, along with the turmeric, a teaspoonful of salt and 700 ml/1¼ pints of water. Bash the lemon grass with a rolling pin to release the flavour, and add that, too, to the pan. Bring to the boil, cover and leave to cook for 35 minutes.

Meanwhile, top and tail the French beans and cut them into 2.5 cm/1 inch lengths; trim and chop the spring onions. Put these into the pan on top of the rice, without stirring, cover and cook for a further 10 minutes, or until the vegetables and rice are tender and all the liquid has been absorbed. Fish out the lemon grass and stir in the lemon juice, which will immediately brighten up the colour of the rice. Stir gently to distribute every-thing, check the seasoning, grind in a bit of pepper, and serve. (Serves 4)

Green Peppers Stuffed with Cauliflower Cheese

These peppers make a good, easy supper dish served with a leafy salad, a tomato salad, or a cooked vegetable. Sometimes, while the peppers are cooking, I make a quick fresh tomato sauce (see overleaf) to serve with them.

4 medium green peppers	200g/7 oz Cheddar cheese,
1 medium cauliflower	grated
	salt and freshly black pepper

Halve the peppers, cutting through their stems. Carefully remove the white inner part and seeds, keeping the stem intact. Put the peppers on a grill pan, shiny-side up, and place them under a hot grill for about 10–15 minutes, until the skin has blistered and begun to char. Remove them from the heat, cover them with a plate to keep in the steam, and leave until they're cool enough to handle.

Meanwhile, wash the cauliflower and cut it into fairly small florets. Cook these in 2.5 cm/1 inch of boiling water, with a lid on the pan, for 4–5 minutes, or until they are just tender. Drain them immediately and put them into a bowl with half the cheese and some salt and pepper.

Slip off the blistered and charred skin from the peppers with a sharp knife – they'll come off easily – then put them on the grill pan. Fill each pepper with the cauliflower cheese mixture, dividing it between them, then sprinkle the rest of the cheese on top of them. Put the peppers under a hot grill for about 10 minutes, or until the cheese is melting, bubbling and golden brown. If serving with the tomato sauce, pour a little on each plate and place the stuffed pepper halves on top. (Serves 4)

To make a fresh tomato sauce, quarter 700g/1½lb of tomatoes and cook them in a dry saucepan, covered, for about 15 minutes or until they're collapsed, then liquidize and sieve them, and season with salt and pepper.

Braised Spring Vegetables and Herbs

You can use a mixture of whatever tender spring vegetables are available: new carrots, baby courgettes, baby turnips, early French beans, shallots and, nicest of all if you can get them, some of those baby artichokes about the size of large rosebuds that you can eat in their entirety. I like to serve this feast of vegetables as a main course, perhaps starting the meal with a soup, or ending with a protein-rich pudding such as Hot Lemon Soufflé (see page 30).

1.2kg/2½ lb young vegetables
2 tbls olive oil
fresh thyme and parsley sprigs

salt and freshly ground black
pepper
2 tbls chopped fresh herbs

Prepare the vegetables, scrubbing rather than scraping them if they're really tender, and cutting them as necessary, aiming for pieces of roughly similar size. Baby artichokes, if you're using these, need any tough leaves trimming off; halve or quarter them unless they're really tiny. Quick-cooking vegetables like baby courgettes can be left whole or added towards the end of the cooking time.

Heat the oil in a large, heavy-based pan with a lid, then put in the vegetables which will take the longest: baby artichokes, followed by fennel, onions, turnips and carrots. Stir them so that they get coated with the oil, add the sprigs of thyme and parsley and salt and pepper, then pour in 100 ml/3½ fl oz of water. Bring to the boil, cover and leave to cook over a gentle heat for a few minutes, until they are almost tender. Artichoke hearts may take up to 20 minutes, but the other vegetables may take as little as 4 minutes.

When they are almost tender, add quick-cooking vegetables

such as courgettes, spring onions, French beans, mangetouts or cauliflower. Stir again, cover and cook for a few minutes longer until all the vegetables are just tender, and bathed in a very little liquid. Fish out the herbs, check the seasoning, sprinkle with the chopped fresh herbs and serve. (Serves 2 as a main course, 4 as a side dish)

Pasta Primavera

A real celebration of spring and, to be honest, early summer, this is one of my favourite pasta dishes. It's well worth taking the trouble to pop the broad beans out of their skins – for the vibrant green colour, apart from anything else! If you're doubtful about the wholewheat noodles in this recipe, I can only urge you to try them; I don't think you'll be disappointed.

450g/1 lb broad beans, about 175g/6 oz after podding
125g/4 oz mangetout peas
225g/8 oz asparagus
25g/1 oz butter
1 garlic clove, crushed
salt and freshly ground black pepper
175g/6 oz wholewheat noodles
a few sprigs of flat-leaf parsley

Pod the beans; top and tail the mangetouts; break any tough ends of the asparagus, wash it well and cut into 2.5 cm/1 inch lengths. Cook the broad beans in fast-boiling water to cover for 2 or 3 minutes, or until the beans are tender. Strain the beans, keeping the liquid. Rinse the beans under cold water to cool them and, with your finger and thumb, pop them out of their grey skins. Re-boil the water the broad beans were cooked in and boil the mangetouts for 30 seconds and then drain them; re-boil the water and cook the asparagus for about 2 minutes, or until it is just tender. (This water makes excellent stock for soups.)

Melt the butter in a large pan and add the garlic; fry for a minute or two, but don't get it brown. Add all the vegetables, and some salt and pepper, cover and leave on one side while you cook the noodles. Bring a large panful of water to the boil, drop in the noodles and bring the water back to the boil. Then draw the pan off the heat, cover and leave for 4–5 minutes until the noodles are just tender but not soggy. Give them a stir and drain them.

While the noodles are cooking, re-heat the vegetables, then add them and their buttery juices to the noodles. Mix gently, season with salt and pepper, add the parsley sprigs, and serve immediately, on to warmed plates. (Serves 2)

If you don't like the idea of wholewheat noodles, use long thin pasta such as fettucine, spaghettini or vermicelli.

Deep-Fried Parmesan-Coated Camembert with Spring Broccoli

The unusual thing about this recipe is the Parmesan coating, which makes it a suitable dish for food combiners. This is usually served as a starter, but I love it as a main course – the lightly cooked spring broccoli goes particularly well with the gooey inside of the cheese. I don't like a sweet sauce with it myself, but if you disagree, try using some delicious all-fruit apricot and peach no-added-sugar jam, gently warmed in a saucepan. I've given quantities for two people here; simply double them for four.

1 x 250g/9 oz Camembert in individual portions	40g/1½ oz ready-grated Parmesan cheese
2 eggs, beaten	450g/1 lb broccoli

First prepare the Camembert: dip each portion into the beaten eggs then into the ready-grated Parmesan, making sure each one is completely coated. This can be done in advance – chill the Camembert in the fridge until about 5 minutes before you want to serve the meal.

Get the broccoli ready in advance, too: remove any tough stems and break or cut the broccoli as necessary. Have ready a large saucepan with 5 cm/2 inches of boiling water for cooking the broccoli, and a pan of hot deep fat for the Camembert. The fat should be 180°C/350°F or hot enough for a cube of bread to rise to the surface immediately and become golden brown in 1 minute.

Put the Camembert into the fat and let it fry for about 5 minutes, or until it is golden brown and crisp all over. At the same time, put the broccoli into the pan of water and cook, covered, for 4–5 minutes, or until just tender. Remove the Camembert from the fat with a slotted spoon and put on to two warmed plates along with the cooked broccoli. Serve immediately. (Serves 2)

A VARIETY OF EGGS

&

Egg Salad Mimosa

This springtime starter – or it could make a lovely light lunch dish – tastes as refreshing as it looks.

2 hard-boiled eggs
½ cucumber
2 tbls wine vinegar
2 tbls olive oil
salt

1 tbls chopped fresh dill
1 small lettuce, an ordinary one
   is fine
½ packet or bunch of watercress
sprigs of fresh dill

Halve the eggs and remove the yolks. Finely chop the yolks and the whites, keeping them separate. Peel and thinly slice the cucumber; put it into a shallow dish and sprinkle with the vinegar, the olive oil, a little salt and 1 tablespoon of chopped dill. Wash and dry the lettuce and watercress. All this can be done in advance.

Just before you want to serve the salad, put a few lettuce leaves on four plates, tearing the larger leaves as necessary, then arrange the rest of the ingredients attractively on top. Garnish with some fresh dill sprigs. (Serves 4)

Stuffed Lightly Curried Eggs

These make quite a filling starter or, served with a spring salad, a good light lunch or supper.

4 eggs, hard-boiled
2 tbls olive oil
2 onions, peeled and finely chopped
2 tsp curry powder
50g/2 oz finely grated Cheddar cheese

1 tbls milk or cream
salt and freshly ground black pepper
300ml/½ pint plain low fat yogurt
dash of sugar (optional)
1–2 tbls snipped chives

Remove the shells from the eggs and keep the eggs on one side for the moment. Heat the oil in a medium pan and put in the onions; fry for 4–5 minutes, or until tender and very lightly browned, then stir in the curry powder and cook for a further minute. Remove from the heat and put half the mixture into a medium bowl.

Cut the eggs in half and scoop out the yolks without damaging the whites. Add the yolks to the onion mixture in the bowl, together with the grated cheese, milk or cream and salt and pepper to taste; mix to a thick, soft consistency. Spoon a little of this mixture into the egg whites.

Add the yogurt to the rest of the onion mixture in the bowl, mix well, then season with salt, pepper and perhaps a tiny dash of sugar. Pour a little of the yogurt sauce mixture on to four small serving dishes, put two of the stuffed eggs on each plate beside or just on top of the sauce, and sprinkle each egg with snipped chives. (Serves 4)

Frittata with Baby Carrots and Spring Onions

You can use any tender spring vegetables for this easy and filling dish. When they come into season, asparagus or baby artichokes are particularly good. This frittata is also very good cold – a picnic food which you can eat with your fingers.

225g/8 oz spring onions
225g/8 oz baby carrots
4 eggs

4 tbls freshly grated Pecorino or
    Parmesan cheese
2 tbls olive oil

Trim the spring onions and chop them into quite small pieces; scrub the carrots and cut them as necessary – if they are very tiny, they can be left whole. Steam or boil the carrots until they are just tender; the time will vary according to how young they are, but it could be as little as 4 minutes. Don't let them get soggy. A minute or two before they're done, put in the spring onions and cook them very briefly, until they, too, are just tender. Drain immediately – the water will make good stock.

Whisk the eggs and add the grated cheese. Have the grill heating up in case you need it. Heat the oil in a large frying pan and put in the drained vegetables; stir-fry them for a minute, then pour in the beaten eggs, moving the vegetables around gently to make sure the egg mixture gets right through them, and that the grated cheese is well distributed. Let the frittata cook over a moderate heat for a few minutes until the underside is cooked and lightly browned. Then, if the top is set, turn the frittata out on to a large plate and back into the frying pan, so that the other side gets cooked. If the top isn't set by the time the underside is done, pop the frying pan under the grill for about half a minute, then turn the frittata out and put it back in the frying pan as described. Cook for a minute or two longer, until the second side is set and lightly browned, cut the frittata into wedges and serve from the pan. (Serves 2)

Rocket Salad

Rocket is one of those herbs which really wakes up your taste buds, and I wish it were more widely available, in good-sized bunches. Anyway, once you've procured some, wash it, tear it into pieces and put into a salad bowl with 1 tablespoon good wine vinegar, 3 tablespoons olive oil, salt and pepper, and some other salad leaves, depending on how much rocket you've been able to get. A fairly neutral leaf, like floppy lettuce, is best, providing a neutral base for the flavour of the rocket.

Swiss Chard Quiche

Swiss chard, with its juicy stems, tender leaves and delicate flavour, makes an excellent quiche, but if you can't get it you could substitute ordinary spinach, using both the leaves and stems.

FOR THE PASTRY
125g/4 oz plain fine wholewheat
    flour
salt
70g/2½ oz butter
1 egg yolk

FOR THE FILLING
225g/8 oz Swiss chard
25g/1 oz butter
220ml/7 fl oz cream
3 egg yolks
salt and freshly ground black
    pepper
grated nutmeg

First set the oven to 200°C/400°C/Gas Mark 6, then make the pastry. Sift the flour into a bowl or food processor and add a good pinch of salt. Put in the butter and either rub it in with your fingers, or whizz in the food processor for a few seconds; add the egg yolk and a teaspoonful of water and mix to a dough. Roll this out on a lightly floured board, then slide it from the board on to a 20 cm/8 inch flan tin, pressing it lightly into the tin to form a case; trim the edges. Prick the base very lightly and bake for 15 minutes, or until the pastry is crisp. Remove from the oven and turn the heat down to 160°C/325°F/Gas Mark 3.

Meanwhile, make the filling. Wash the Swiss chard, separate the stalks from the leaves, and chop both. Melt the butter in a saucepan, put in the stalks, cover and cook for about 4 minutes, or until they are almost tender. Put in the leaves, cover and cook for a further 2–3 minutes, or until everything is tender. Remove from the heat and mix in the cream, add the egg yolks, salt, pepper and nutmeg to taste, stirring well. Pour the mixture into the flan case and bake for 25–30 minutes, or until the filling is set. Serve hot, warm or cold. (Serves 4–6)

The Swiss chard quiche, above, is most delicious made with cream, but for a less rich version use milk or a mixture of milk and cream.

Savoury Spinach Gateau

I invented this for a special meal and it brought gasps of delight when it appeared. It's not difficult to make although you do need a food processor.

FOR THE GATEAU
1.4kg/3 lb fresh spinach or
    700g/1½ lb frozen
25g/1 oz butter
4 egg yolks
salt and freshly ground black
    pepper
8 egg whites
6 tbls ready-grated Parmesan
    cheese

FOR THE FILLING
1 medium cauliflower, yielding
    450g/1 lb florets
225g/8 oz butter
4 egg yolks
2 tbls lemon juice
salt
chervil sprigs to garnish

Set the oven to 200°C/400°F/Gas Mark 6. Line the base of three 20 cm/8 inch sandwich tins with non-stick paper, and grease the sides. If you only have two such tins, cut a circle of paper for the third, bake two of the gâteaux, then turn one out, re-line and grease the tin, and bake the third.

If you're using fresh spinach, wash it well, then put it into a large saucepan and cook over a high heat for 7–10 minutes, or until very tender. Cook frozen spinach in a little boiling water, also for about 7 minutes. In either case, drain the spinach into a colander and press it very well to extract as much water as possible. Then put it into a food processor, along with the butter, egg yolks, salt and freshly ground pepper, and whizz it to a smooth, creamy purée.

Whisk the egg whites until they stand in stiff peaks, then gently fold into the spinach mixture. Tip a third of the mixture into each of the tins, level the tops, then sprinkle each with 2 tablespoons of the grated Parmesan. Bake for 10 minutes, until they are golden brown on top and the centres feel firm. (If you are baking them in two batches, turn one of the gâteaux straight out, cheesy-side down, on to a large round ovenproof serving plate, re-line the tin and bake the remaining gâteau.) When they are all done, reduce the oven setting to 160°C/325°F/Gas Mark 3.

While the gâteaux are cooking, wash and trim the cauliflower, cutting it into quite small florets. Steam the cauliflower, or boil it in 2 cm/1 inch of water until tender and drain well.

Next make the sauce. Cut up the butter roughly, put it into a small saucepan and heat until it has melted and is boiling. Put the egg yolks and lemon juice into a food processor or blender with a good pinch of salt and whizz for 1 minute. With the machine running, pour the melted butter in a steady stream into the food processor or blender through the top of the goblet, and whizz for 1 minute.

Put one layer of the gâteau on an ovenproof serving plate, spread the surface with half the sauce, then put half the cauliflower on top, followed by another layer of gâteau. Cover this with sauce and cauliflower as before, then put the final layer of gâteau on top, this time with the crunchy cheese side on top. Put the gâteau, uncovered, into the oven, and leave it for 30 minutes to heat through completely before serving. Garnish with sprigs of chervil, and serve in wedges, like a cake. (Serves 6–8)

FRUITS, CUSTARDS AND CREAMS

ℰ

Rhubarb Crumble

This, in my experience, is one of those 'spring wouldn't be the same without' kind of puddings. Fortunately, it's also one of the easiest to make. It's good with some cream or thick yogurt.

900g/2 lb rhubarb
50g/2 oz caster sugar
¼ tsp ground cloves
½ tsp ground cinnamon

FOR THE CRUMBLE
175g/6 oz self-raising fine
    wholemeal flour
125g/4 oz soft butter or
    vegetable margarine
125g/4 oz demerara sugar

Set the oven to 200°C/400°F/Gas Mark 6.

Cut the root ends and leafy tops off the rhubarb, then cut the stalks into 2.5 cm/1 inch lengths and put them into a shallow ovenproof dish. Sprinkle them with the caster sugar, ground cloves and cinnamon.

To make the crumble, sift the flour into a bowl, adding the bran from the sieve too. With your fingertips, rub the butter or margarine into the flour until the mixture resembles fine bread-crumbs. Add the sugar and rub lightly again, to form a crumbly mixture. Spoon this on top of the rhubarb in an even layer, covering it completely. Bake for about 30 minutes, or until the crumble is crisp and lightly browned and the rhubarb feels tender when tested through the crumble with the point of a knife. (Serves 4)

Mango and Cardamom Parfait

I love both mango and cardamom, with its eucalyptus-like flavour. Together they make an exquisite icecream parfait which you can freeze in a loaf tin, without stirring, and serve in slices.

1 medium ripe mango
6–8 cardamom pods
4 egg yolks
75g/3 oz caster sugar

150ml/7 fl oz double cream
mango slices and pistachio nuts
to decorate

Peel the mango, cut the flesh into chunks and put into a food processor. Crush the cardamom and remove the pods, then crush the seeds as much as you can, preferably with a pestle and mortar. Add them to the mango, and whizz for a minute or two until you have a completely smooth purée. Pour this through a fairly coarse nylon sieve to remove any larger pieces of cardamom.

Whisk the egg yolks until they are thick. Put the sugar into a small saucepan with 2 tablespoons of water and heat gently until the sugar has dissolved. Then boil for 2–3 minutes, until the mixture reaches 110°C/225°C on a sugar thermometer or a little of the syrup forms a thread when pulled between your finger and thumb. Pour this over the egg yolks, then whisk for 4–5 minutes, until the mixture is very thick and pale. Stir the mango purée into the egg yolk mixture. Whisk the cream until it is thick but not stiff, then fold this in too. Pour the mixture into a 450g/1lb loaf tin and freeze until solid.

Remove the parfait 15 minutes before you want to serve it. Run the blade of a knife around the edges and invert the tin over a plate, giving it a firm shake; it should come out with no problems. Decorate with mango slices and chopped pistachios. (Serves 8)

To slice a mango, cut downwards about 6mm/¼inch from one side of the stem, then slice it the same distance the other side of the stem, thus avoiding the stone. Then remove the skin, and cut as much flesh away from the stone as you can.

Spring Fruit Salad with Violets

This fruit salad makes the most of what fruit there is during spring. It's naturally sweetened with grape juice and is most refreshing: I love to eat it for breakfast, particularly a late and leisurely Sunday one. You probably won't need all the grape juice for the fruit salad, but any that's over is nice to drink with it. (The violets are an optional extra for special occasions.)

1 honeydew melon or similar, or
    part of one if it's huge
4–6 kiwi fruit
225g/8 oz seedless green grapes

1 bottle or carton of white
    grape juice
small bunch of violets

Halve the melon, remove the seeds and cut the flesh into pieces; peel and slice the kiwi fruit; remove the grapes from their stems and wash them. Put all the fruits into a bowl – they look especially good in a glass one – and pour in enough grape juice to moisten them well. Remove some violets from their stems and float them on top of the fruit salad. Serve as soon as possible. (Serves 4)

Little Coffee Creams

I like these best made with mascarpone, which is rich, smooth and very creamy, but thick, Greek yogurt or fromage frais with 8% fat are also good. All of these come in tubs of varying sizes so basically aim for one that's about 200–250g/7–9oz for two people. It doesn't matter whether the coffee is with or without caffeine as long as it's a good quality one.

225g/8oz mascarpone, Greek
    yogurt or fromage frais
2 tsp good-quality strong instant
    coffee

2 heaped tsp sugar
sugar coffee beans to decorate
    (optional)

Put the mascarpone, yogurt or fromage frais into a bowl and stir a little to make it smooth. Put the coffee granules into a cup and add about a tablespoonful of almost-boiling water – just enough to dissolve them. Add the coffee to the bowl, along with the sugar, and stir until it's all well-combined.

Spoon the mixture into two bowls, and chill until you're ready to serve them. Decorate with two or three sugar coffee beans, if you have them. (Serves 2)

For a vegan version of little coffee creams, use either vegan yogurt (from health shops) or silken tofu, whizzed in a food processor.

Spring Fruit Compôte

This delightful compôte is sweetened with all-fruit, apricot and peach soft-set spread instead of sugar. Make sure the pineapple is sweet and ripe; it should smell syrupy, a bit like canned pineapple, and one of the inner leaves should come out quite easily when you pull it. Kiwis are nicest if they give a bit when you press them. I don't think this compôte needs any accompaniments; it's good just as it is, for a pudding or as a special breakfast dish.

1 small ripe pineapple	4 kiwi fruit
350g/12 oz jar of all-fruit apricot and peach soft-set spread	2 eating apples

Cut the leafy top off the pineapple, cut the fruit into quarters and cut the peel and inner core off each quarter. Scoop out any 'eyes' with the point of a knife, then cut the fruit into chunky pieces and put them in a bowl with the apricot and peach spread, mixing well. Peel the kiwis and slice them into thin rounds; peel, core and slice the apples. Add these to the bowl and stir gently.

Cover and leave for at least 30 minutes, preferably 1–2 hours, for the flavours to blend. (Serves 4)

Hot Lemon Soufflé with Apricot Coulis

This makes a good springtime pudding, hot and warming for still-chilly days but at the same time light and refreshing. The base can be prepared in advance, leaving only the whisking and folding-in of the egg whites to be done before you pop it into the oven. It's good served with pouring cream and perhaps some seasonal fruits, and especially marvellous with the coulis.

25g/1 oz butter plus a little for greasing
25g/1 oz flour
200ml/7 fl oz milk
50g/2 oz caster sugar

grated rind of 2 lemons
1 tbls lemon juice
3 egg yolks
4 egg whites

Use the extra butter to grease a 1 L/1¾ pint soufflé dish. Tie a piece of non-stick paper around the outside of the dish to extend by 5 cm/2 inches or so, to allow the soufflé to rise above the top of the dish.

Melt the remaining butter in a medium saucepan. When it froths, stir in the flour, cook over the heat for a moment or two and add the milk, stirring until it forms a smooth paste. Add the sugar, lemon rind and juice, then leave on one side until you are ready to finish the soufflé.

Set the oven to 160°C/325°F/Gas Mark 3. Gently reheat the flour mixture just to soften it, but don't get it too hot, then remove it from the heat and stir in the egg yolks. Whisk the egg whites until they stand in stiff peaks. Mix a heaped tablespoon of egg white into the flour mixture to loosen it, then fold in the rest of the egg white. Pour the mixture into the soufflé dish, gently level the top, then run your thumb or a knife round the top edge to remove the soufflé from the edges of the dish and help it to rise well. Bake the soufflé for 30–35 minutes, or until it has risen well and just wobbles a little in the centre when shaken. Remove the band of paper and serve immediately, with the Apricot Coulis. (Serves 4)

Apricot Coulis

Put 225g/8oz dried apricots into a saucepan, cover with plenty of water and leave to soak overnight. Next day, add 25g/1oz sugar, a vanilla pod if you have one, and more water if necessary so that the apricots are well covered. Bring to the boil, then let them simmer, uncovered, for about an hour until nearly all the water has gone and the apricots are very tender and bathed in a glossy syrup. Cool, then remove the vanilla pod (wash it and leave it to dry, to be used again). Liquidize the apricots thoroughly, adding a little water if the mixture is very thick. Serve in a jug, with the soufflé.

Apricot coulis freezes well, so it's useful to make extra and freeze in suitably sized containers.

Chocolate Mousse with Orange Cream

Cold, velvety-smooth, rich chocolate with a topping of orange-flavoured whipped cream makes an irresistible finale to any meal. It needs to be made several hours before you want to eat – even the day before.

200g/7 oz plain chocolate,
    at least 50% cocoa solids
25g/1 oz butter
5 eggs
1 orange

150ml/5 fl oz whipping cream
1 tbs Cointreau or other orange
    liqueur
caster sugar

Break up the chocolate and put it into a large bowl with the butter. Stand the bowl over a saucepan of gently simmering water and leave for about 10 minutes until the chocolate has melted. Meanwhile, separate the eggs, putting the whites into a large bowl and the yolks into a small one.

Whisk the whites until they are stiff but not breaking up. Remove the bowl of chocolate from the pan and stir in the egg yolks, followed by a good tablespoonful of the egg white. Then tip in the rest of the egg white and fold it in very gently using a metal spoon, until there is no more white to be seen and the mixture is light and fluffy. Pour the mixture into six smallish individual glass dishes or ramekins and put into the fridge to set and chill for 6 hours or more.

Just before you want to serve the chocolate mousse, prepare the orange topping. First, scrub the orange in hot water, then with a zester remove several long strands of rind for decoration; grate the rest to make about ¼ teaspoonful. Whisk the cream until it holds its shape, add the grated orange rind, Cointreau and a little caster sugar to taste and whisk lightly again. Spoon this mixture on top of the chocolate mousse and decorate with the strands of orange rind. (Serves 6)

Florida Fruit Cup

A taste of sunshine to cheer up chilly spring days, this fruit cup is made from the tropical fruits which are good at this time of the year, and you can vary the exact composition according to what's available. The pink grapefruit makes a pleasant addition, and the passion fruit permeate the whole dish with their exotic flavour. It makes a particularly wonderful brunch offering – but it's good any time.

1 large pink grapefruit	225g/8 oz lychees
2 oranges	1 ripe mango
125g/4 oz seedless grapes	2 passion fruit
2 apples	

Holding the grapefruit over a bowl, cut off the peel in one long strip using a sawing action and making sure that you cut off the white pith as well as the skin. Cut the flesh away from between the white transparent membranes and, when you've removed all the flesh, squeeze out any remaining juice. Do the same thing with the oranges, then wash the grapes and add these to the bowl; wash and slice the apples, removing their skin or not according to its condition. Remove first the skin and then the shiny brown stones from the lychees using a sharp, pointed knife, and add the lychees to the bowl. Cut right down the mango on both sides of the big flat stone, starting about 5 mm/¼ inch each side of the stalk. Peel and slice the flesh, cutting away as much as you can from around the stone and adding that too. Finally, cut the passion fruit in half and scoop out the flesh, including the pips, with a teaspoon; add this to the other fruit and stir gently. Cover until needed.

It's best made half an hour or so before you want to eat it, to give the flavours a chance to blend and the juices to run, making a natural syrup. (Serves 4–6)

SPRING MENUS

&

Menu

DINNER
FRESH FROM THE GARDEN
FOR FOUR

CREAM OF TURNIP SOUP
HOT HERB BREAD

TWICE-BAKED INDIVIDUAL SOUFFLÉS
CREAMY TOMATO SAUCE
PLATTER OF FRESH VEGETABLES

SPICED RHUBARB COMPÔTE WITH
BROWN SUGAR MERINGUES

Countdown

Up To One Week In Advance
❑ Make the meringues which can be kept in an air-tight container.

Up To One Day Before
❑ The following dishes can be made in advance, covered and kept in the fridge: the soup; the herb bread, prepared ready for cooking and wrapped in foil; the Twice-Baked Soufflés, turned out into a casserole dish ready for their final baking; the Tomato Sauce; the Rhubarb Compôte. If you are going to microwave the vegetable platter, this can also be cooked, covered and kept in the fridge.

40 Minutes Before The Meal
❑ Heat the oven. Put in the herb bread 20 minutes before you want to eat it; 5 minutes later put in the Soufflés. Gently reheat the soup and sauce; just before you want to serve the meal reheat the vegetables in the microwave or cook them if you haven't done so already.

Cream of Turnip Soup

If the turnips really are 'fresh from the garden', some or all of the leafy green tops can be used in this soup too; if not, add some watercress, to give pungency.

450g/1 lb turnips, plus 75g/3 oz of the leaves, or watercress	salt and freshly ground black pepper
1 onion, peeled and chopped	grated nutmeg
15g/½ oz butter	extra cream and chopped chives
4 tbls double cream	to garnish

Scrub the turnips and cut them into even-sized dice; wash and roughly chop the leaves or watercress. Melt the butter in a large saucepan and put in the onion; cover and cook for 5 minutes, then add the turnips and the green tops or watercress and cook, covered, for a further 5 minutes. Pour in 850 ml/1½ pints of water, bring to the boil and simmer for about 20 minutes, or until the vegetables are tender.

Liquidize the soup thoroughly, then pour it back into the saucepan and stir in the cream, salt, pepper and nutmeg to taste. To serve, garnish with cream and chopped chives.

Hot Herb Bread

You can use whatever herbs are available; a few fresh chives and a bit of thyme, if you can get it, otherwise just some dried thyme.

1 wholewheat or Granary stick 75g/3 oz butter	1 tbls chopped fresh chives and a sprig of fresh thyme, chopped, or ½ tsp dried thyme

Make diagonal cuts in the wholewheat or Granary stick about 2.5 cm/1 inch apart, without cutting right through the bottom crust of the bread. Beat the butter until it's soft, then mix in the chives and thyme or the dried thyme. Spread the cut surfaces of the bread with the herb butter, then wrap the bread in foil – you may need to break the loaf in half so that it will fit into the oven.

Bake the bread for 15–20 minutes in a hot oven – it will bake perfectly with the soufflés – until the butter has melted and the bread is very hot. Serve at once, with the soup.

Twice-Baked Individual Soufflés

This is my food-combining version of this modern classic, using curd cheese or skim milk cheese for the base instead of the usual thick sauce, to make a completely protein dish. It's very convenient, because everything can be done in advance except for the final baking of the soufflés. They can even be made and frozen in their dish, ready to be quickly defrosted and baked.

butter for greasing
8 tbls ready-grated Parmesan
  cheese
225g/8 oz curd or skim milk
  cheese
4 egg yolks

150g/5 oz Gruyère cheese,
  grated
5 egg whites
salt and freshly ground black
  pepper

Set the oven to 180°C/350°F/Gas Mark 4. Generously grease eight ramekins, dariole moulds or old cups, then sprinkle the insides with Parmesan, using 4 tablespoons. Put the curd or skim milk cheese into a bowl and mash it until it's smooth, then gradually mix in the egg yolks and half the grated Gruyère cheese. Whisk the egg whites with a clean, greasefree whisk until they are standing in peaks, and stir a heaped tablespoonful into the egg yolk mixture to loosen it. Fold in the rest of the egg whites gently. Spoon the mixture into the ramekins, moulds or cups: it can come level with the top, but don't pile it up any higher.

Stand them in a roasting tin, pour boiling water round to come halfway up the sides and bake for 15 minutes, until they are risen and set. Remove from the oven and leave to get cold – they'll sink a bit. Loosen the edges and turn them out. (It's easiest to turn them out to your hand, then transfer them to an ovenproof serving dish.) Sprinkle each with some of the remaining Gruyère cheese then with the rest of the Parmesan cheese.

They can now wait until you are ready to bake them. Then, heat the oven to 220°C/425°F/Gas Mark 7, and bake them for 15–20 minutes, or until they are puffed up and golden brown. Serve at once.

Creamy Tomato Sauce

1 tbls olive oil
1 small onion, peeled and finely
  chopped
900g/2 lb tomatoes

salt and freshly ground black
  pepper
4 tbls cream

Heat the oil in a large saucepan and add the onion; fry for 5 minutes without browning. Meanwhile, quarter the tomatoes and add them to the pan. Cover and cook over a gentle heat for 10–15 minutes, or until the tomatoes have collapsed, then liquidize, sieve and season. Just before you want to serve the sauce, re-heat it gently and add the cream. Check the seasoning, then serve.

Platter of Fresh Vegetables

A platter of fresh baby vegetables is one of the joys of late spring and early summer. The exact composition is up to you – and your garden or supplier – this is just a suggestion. Trim and cut the vegetables as little as possible and cook until they're just tender.

175g/6 oz baby carrots
175g/6 oz baby turnips
175g/6 oz baby French beans
175g/6 oz baby courgettes
175g/6 oz sugar-snap peas
2–3 baby cauliflowers,

depending on the size
50g/2 oz butter
2 tbls fresh lemon juice
salt and freshly ground black
  pepper
chopped fresh parsley

Wash and gently scrub the carrots and turnips, leaving some of the green leaves still attached. Wash, top and tail the French beans, baby courgettes and sugar-snap peas; wash, trim and quarter the cauliflowers (or cut them as necessary, depending on the size). The easiest way to cook a variety of vegetables like this is in a steamer – or a stack of steamers – over a large saucepan of water, since you can add the vegetables in sequence according to how long they'll take. This saves having to use several saucepans. The exact timing depends on the size of the vegetables, but if they're young and tender, none of them will take more than about 4 minutes at the most. If you wish, you can cook them separately, in advance, under-cooking them slightly, then put them into a vegetable dish, cover with a plate and microwave them just before serving.

When the vegetables are cooked, quickly melt the butter in a saucepan with the lemon juice and a good seasoning of salt and pepper, then pour this over the cooked vegetables; sprinkle with some chopped parsley just before you serve them.

Spiced Rhubarb Compôte

This easy-to-make recipe is a particularly good way to use the new season's rhubarb, and is delicious with the crunchy Brown Sugar Meringues below.

900g/2 lb rhubarb	8 cloves
50g/2 oz caster sugar	good pinch of ground ginger

Trim the rhubarb and strip off any stringy bits then cut into 2.5 cm/1 inch lengths and put into a heavy-based saucepan with the sugar, 4 tablespoons of water, the cloves and ginger. Cover and cook over a gentle heat for about 5 minutes, or until soft. Transfer the rhubarb to a bowl, removing the cloves as you do so, cover and chill.

Serve with the brown sugar meringues, and, if wished, some softly whipped cream.

Brown Sugar Meringues

The brown sugar in these meringues gives them a pleasant caramel-like flavour.

2 egg whites   50g/2 oz dark brown sugar
50g/2 oz caster sugar

Set the oven to 70°C/150°F/Gas Mark ¼ or to your lowest setting. Line a baking sheet with non-stick paper. Whisk the egg whites until they are very stiff. Now whisk in first the caster sugar, then the dark brown sugar, a little at a time, whisking well to make a glossy mixture. Shape spoonfuls of the mixture on to the baking sheet, leaving some space around them as they spread a little. Bake them for 2–3 hours, or until they are dry and crisp. Pick one up and look at the base of it to make sure that it is dry right through. Cool on the baking sheet then store them in an airtight container.

A good wine to accompany this menu would be an aromatic dry white such as Sancerre, or a medium-bodied red such as a Red Burgundy.

§

Menu

A LATE SPRING
PICNIC FOR FOUR

LIGHT LEEK SOUP

TIAN OF SPRING VEGETABLES WITH
SPECIAL MAYONNAISE

SALADE NICOISE WITH NEW POTATOES
AND SPRING ONIONS

LITTLE LEMON GRASS CREAMS

———————————

Up To One Day Before

❑ The soup, Tian, Special Mayonnaise and Lemon Grass Creams can be made in advance, covered securely in foil and kept in the fridge if convenient. You can also cook the potatoes, beans and hardboiled eggs for the salad, ready to assemble it on the day.

On The Day

❑ Reheat the soup gently and put into a vacuum flask; complete the salad, put into a suitable container or bowl and cover securely with foil.

Light Leek Soup

In my experience, unless you're very lucky with the weather a soup makes the most welcome starter on a late spring picnic – and on many a summer one, too. This one is made from the last of the leeks. Take it in Thermos flasks and serve it into cups or bowls, whichever are most convenient. It's helpful to have spoons, too, to get up the last dregs of the delicious mixture. If the weather does happen to be boiling hot, by the way, this soup is also good served chilled.

700g/1 ½ lb leeks
1 tbls olive oil
1.2L/2 pints water
4 tbls cream

salt and freshly ground black pepper
freshly grated nutmeg

Trim the roots and inedible leaf parts off the leeks, then slit them up one side and rinse under the running cold tap, pulling them open to make sure you get them really clean. Cut in half downwards, down again, and then across thinly, resulting in quite small pieces.

Heat the olive oil in a large saucepan and put in the leeks, stir then cover and let them cook very gently for 10 minutes, stirring a couple of times. Add the water and let the soup simmer for about 20 minutes, or until the leeks are very tender. Liquidize about two-thirds of the soup – leave the rest as it is to add texture. Stir in the cream and season the soup well with salt, black pepper and freshly grated nutmeg. If you want to eat it hot, pour into Thermos flasks immediately; if cold, cool first then pack into flasks.

Tian of Spring Vegetables with Special Mayonnaise

I'm particularly fond of this easy, economical dish which can be made from any combination of seasonal vegetables, although I prefer it when some leafy green ones are included. The fresh herbs, too, can be varied according to what is available – I particularly like the flavour of fresh dill. It's good served either hot with some cooked vegetables and perhaps a tomato or yogurt sauce or, as suggested here, cold with mayonnaise (or a yogurt sauce) and a tomato and basil salad.

bunch of spring onions	2 eggs
450g/1 lb courgettes	2 tbls chopped fresh herbs
225g/8 oz Swiss chard or spinach	salt and freshly ground black
125g/4 oz button mushrooms	pepper
2 tbls olive oil	25g/1 oz freshly grated
	Parmesan cheese

Set the oven to 180°C/350°F/Gas Mark 4. Wash and trim the spring onions and courgettes, then slice the onions and cut the courgettes into small dice. Wash the chard or spinach, removing the stems and chop both the stems and the leaves, keeping them separate. Rinse and halve the mushrooms.

Heat the oil in a large saucepan and put in the spring onions, courgettes and chard or spinach stems. Cover and cook for 5 minutes, then add the chard or spinach leaves and the button mushrooms and cook for a further 5 minutes, without a lid.

Remove the pan from the heat and beat in the eggs, then add the herbs and salt and pepper to taste. Spoon the mixture into one shallow ovenproof dish or four smaller ones, spread the top level and sprinkle with the Parmesan cheese. Bake for about 30 minutes for the large dish or 20 minutes for the smaller dishes, or until set and lightly browned. Serve hot or cold.

Special Mayonnaise

You could use a good-quality bought mayonnaise jazzed up a bit with some lemon juice and freshly ground black pepper for the Tian, but a home-made one is nicer if you have the time to make it. I think that this is rather a special recipe because, although it looks and tastes like a perfectly straight-forward mayonnaise, it does not contain egg yolk. The original idea came to me when I was experimenting with vegan mayonnaises (you can make this recipe vegan by using soya milk instead of the cream), and then I realized how useful it would be for anyone worried about salmonella. It's a bit easier to make than a normal mayonnaise, because you don't have to be quite so careful about adding the oil, but it's still best to do this quite slowly until the mayonnaise shows signs of thickening. It will keep, well-covered, for a week in the fridge.

4 tbls single cream
¼ tsp mustard powder
salt and freshly ground black
  pepper

200ml/7 fl oz light olive oil,
  grapeseed or groundnut oil
1 tbls lemon juice
1 tbls red wine vinegar

Put the single cream into a bowl with the mustard powder and a good seasoning of salt and pepper, and mix them together. Add the oil gradually, a drop at a time, whisking well after each addition, exactly as if you were making an egg-yolk mayonnaise. When about half the oil has been added and the mixture has emulsified, you can add the rest more quickly in a thin, steady stream, but still whisking all the time. Finally, add the lemon juice and vinegar and stir them in very gently in one direction only, which will further thicken the mixture because of the effect of the acid on the cream. Check the seasoning – this mayonnaise needs plenty of salt and pepper.

Should the mayonnaise curdle as you're making it, you can easily remedy the situation if you start again with a tablespoon of cream in a clean bowl and whisk in the curdled mixture a bit at a time. I have just done exactly this when I was testing this recipe, and it's fine!

Salade Nicoise with New Potatoes and Spring Onions

450g/1 lb new potatoes, scrubbed
225g/8 oz young French beans
2 tbls red wine vinegar
6 tbls olive oil
salt and freshly ground black
  pepper

4 tomatoes
4 hard-boiled eggs, shelled
bunch of spring onions
50–125g/2–4 oz black olives

Cook the potatoes in enough boiling water to cover for 10–15 minutes, or until they are just tender; drain them. Top and tail the French beans as necessary and cook them in 2.5 cm/1 inch of boiling water for 2–4 minutes, or until they, too are just tender then drain them. Put the vinegar, oil and some salt and pepper into a large bowl, put in the potatoes and beans, turn gently so that they are all coated with the dressing, and leave to cool.

Cut the tomatoes and eggs into quarters or eighths and chop the spring onions. Add these to the bowl, together with the olives, and stir gently. Serve cold.

Little Lemon Grass Creams

Every year a national supermarket holds a nationwide contest to find the best young cooks between the ages of 9 and 15, and very inspiring it is. At one of the regional finals which I attended, one of the competitors, Caroline Godsmark, made some exquisite lemon grass creams which all the judges loved, and it is from her that I got the idea for this fragrant desert.

3 lemon grass	2 eggs and 2 egg yolks
150ml/5 fl oz milk	40g/1½ oz caster sugar
150ml/5 fl oz single cream	herb flowers such as sage to decorate

Set the oven to 160°C/325°F/Gas Mark 3.

Put the lemon grass on a board and bash it with a rolling pin to crush it and release the flavour. Put the crushed lemon grass into a saucepan with the milk and cream and bring to the boil, then cover and leave for 15 minutes for the flavour to infuse.

Meanwhile, whisk the eggs and egg yolks with the sugar until frothy but not thick. Remove the lemon grass from the milk and cream and bring back to the boil, then pour them over the egg and sugar mixture. Strain this into four individual ramekins and put them into a roasting tin. Cover with foil, pour boiling water around them to come two-thirds up the sides of the ramekins, and bake for about 40–45 minutes until the custards are set.

Remove them from the oven, take them out of the tin and leave to cool. Decorate with herb flowers before serving.

A light or medium-bodied dry white wine such as Frascati, Chablis or Muscadet goes well with this menu, with plenty of still or sparkling water or fruit juice as an alternative.

SUMMER

⅋

SUMMER

&

With the sun moving daily towards its highest point above the the horizon, the days become even longer and sunnier, and the evenings are now warm and light. There is a feeling of relaxation and conviviality as we spend more time outside, making contact with other people, enjoying the fresh air and the sights and sounds of summer. The summer solstice marks midsummer when the sun reaches its zenith, and for me there is something especially magical about this time of year; it is a time of celebration for all the benefits bestowed by the sun to life on earth, demonstrated by the burgeoning growth and fruiting of plants all around us.

Summer vegetables are mainly light and juicy; courgettes, tomatoes, delicate summer spinach, tender young peas, fennel, many varieties of salad leaf and, of course, home-grown asparagus, for me one of the peaks of the culinary calendar for its short season which, where I live, lasts from the end of May until midsummer's day, although imported asparagus continues to be available after that. Summer fruits, too, have a high water content, to quench thirst and refresh parched throats. Perhaps the watermelon, much-loved in hot countries, is the best example of this, but soft fruits such as strawberries, raspberries and red, white and blackcurrants, not to mention peaches and nectarines, are also freely available, juicy and cooling. They form the basis of some delectable summer puddings and can make a light meal in themselves – in the intense heat they may be the only thing you fancy. Strawberries, in particular, still say 'summer' to me, even though I see them in my local super-market all the year round. And edible flowers such as rose, nasturtiums, marigolds, borage, pinks and lavender can be used for flavour and decoration, underlying the delicacy of summer foods.

For high summer, chilled or iced soups and starters make a tempting start to a meal, refreshing a hot and jaded palate. Light, easy vegetable-based dishes and summer pastas and grains make tempting main courses; dishes such as the Stuffed Courgettes with Fresh Tomato Sauce (page 60), Summer Spaghetti (page 62), Tomatoes Stuffed with Flageolet Beans (pages 66–7). Herbs are of course abundant and a delightful way of adding a variety of flavours to many dishes, including salads. Light, juicy fruit and vegetables mean quicker cooking, or none at all, giving more time to spend outside. We eat in the garden at every possible opportunity, often just carrying our plates of food outside to eat sitting on the lawn or having a barbecue, vege-tarian style, which is easy, as the menu on pages 82–9 shows. It's great, too, that the habit of eating outside in restaurants, pubs and street cafés is more popular these days.

As summer advances, the foods begin to get a little more substantial; left alone, courgettes turn into vegetable marrows, runner beans grow with speed and need frequent picking, home-grown peppers, aubergines and mature artichokes become avail-able. Blackberries weigh down the hedgerows, free for the picking, and purple bilberries can be found on the moors, bringing more delectable flavours and possibilities for menus. Whenever possible, I like to use fruits which are naturally sweet as they are, or that need only small quantities of apple or pear juice concentrate which you can get at health food shops, or real maple syrup; or, in larger quantities, some delectable all-fruit spreads which are made by a major supermarket chain. Sometimes I like to use chocolate, partly as a sweetener and partly for the sheer pleasure of its flavour, but I like to use one with a high cocoa solids content – at least 50 per cent, 60 per cent preferably; read the label. I buy mine from the baking department of the supermarket chain I've already mentioned – and, no, I don't have shares with them!

CHILLED SOUPS AND STARTERS

&

Watermelon and Mint

a good-sized piece of watermelon   8 sprigs of fresh mint

Cut the skin off the watermelon and remove the seeds; cut the flesh into manageable-sized pieces and put them into a bowl. Tear the leaves from four of the mint sprigs and add to the bowl. Mix, then cover and chill until required. Spoon the mixture into four individual dishes – it looks pretty in glass ones – and decorate each with a sprig of mint. (Serves 4)

I enjoy this for its colour as much as anything, although watermelon and mint together make a refreshing combination on a hot day.

Iced Lettuce Soup

900g/2 lb outside lettuce leaves   4 tbls single cream
2 tbls olive oil   salt and freshly ground black
1 onion, peeled and chopped   pepper
2 or 3 sprigs of fresh mint   chopped mint to garnish, and
                                                              extra cream if wished

Wash the lettuce leaves well then shred them. Heat the oil in a large saucepan and put in the onion; cover and cook for 5 minutes, add the lettuce and mint, cover again, and cook for a further 5 minutes. Pour in 850 ml/1½ pints of water, bring to the boil and simmer for about 15 minutes, or until the vegetables are very tender.

Liquidize the soup thoroughly, then pour it through a sieve into a pan. Stir in the cream and season with salt and pepper. Cool, then chill the soup. Serve in bowls, garnished with some chopped mint and a swirl of cream if liked. (Serves 4)

Outside leaves of lettuce which are too tough for a salad are fine for this refreshing soup.

Tomato Sorbet

This tomato sorbet makes a most refreshing starter on a summer's day. You do need a food processor in order to make it.

1 tbls olive oil
1 onion, peeled and chopped
450g/1 lb tomatoes
2 strips of lemon peel
salt and freshly ground black
  pepper

TO SERVE
lettuce leaves
chopped fresh chives or basil

Heat the oil in a large saucepan, add the onion, cover and cook for 5 minutes without browning. Meanwhile, chop the tomatoes roughly (there's no need to skin them) and add them to the pan, along with the lemon peel. Cover and cook gently for a further 15–20 minutes, or until the tomatoes have collapsed to a purée. Remove from the heat, liquidize, lemon peel and all, then pass the mixture through a sieve. Season well with salt and freshly ground black pepper. Pour into a shallow container so that the tomato purée is no more than 1 cm/½ inch thick, cool and freeze.

Just before you want to serve the sorbet, put two or three tender lettuce leaves on four serving plates or glass dishes. Take the sorbet out of the fridge, turn it out on to a chopping board and, with a sharp knife, cut it into small pieces, about 1 cm/ ½ inch square. Put these into the food processor and whizz for a minute or two, until the mixture turns to a smooth ice and holds together. Quickly put scoops of this on the plates, on top of the lettuce. Sprinkle the chopped chives or basil over the top of the ice and serve. (Serves 4)

Stuffed Courgette Flowers

Courgette flowers are not easy to come by unless you grow your own, though sometimes kind friends who grow courgettes will provide them or pick-your-own places will let you pick some if you ask first. If you can get hold of them, they make a delightful light starter, which can be made more substantial by the addition of some fresh tomato sauce (see page 60) if you wish.

125g/4 oz Mozzarella cheese (packed in water)
8 courgette flowers
2 eggs

salt and freshly ground black pepper
ready-grated Parmesan cheese
olive oil
sliced of lemon to serve

Cut the Mozzarella cheese into eight pieces the right size to fit into the courgette flowers. With your fingers, pinch out the stamens from inside the flowers, then put a piece of Mozzarella cheese inside each one. Fold the tips of the petals over so that the cheese is fully enclosed.

Separate the eggs; whisk the whites until they're stiff, then beat the yolks a little to break them up, and fold in the whites. Season with salt and pepper. Holding the courgette flowers by the green baby courgette part, dip the flowers first into the egg mixture, making sure they are completely coated, then into the ready-grated Parmesan cheese. Fry them in a little olive oil, turning them over after a minute or two so that the flowers get brown and crisp all over. (They will only take 3–4 minutes in all to cook.) Drain them on kitchen paper and serve immediately on warmed, individual plates. Garnish each plate with a slice of lemon. (Serves 4)

Broad Bean Pâté with Grilled Fennel

I think that this pâté is best if you take the time to pop the beans out of their skins first, although you can make it without doing this – in which case it will have a more chewy texture. If you don't want to do the fennel, some bread would also go well with it.

450g/1 lb shelled broad beans
25g/1 oz butter
2 tbls lemon juice
salt and freshly ground black
  pepper

2 fennel bulbs
olive oil
1 tbls red wine vinegar
black olives

Cook the broad beans in boiling water for a few minutes until they are done, then drain them. With your finger and thumb, pop them out of their grey skins; discard the skins. Put the beans into a food processor with the butter, lemon juice and some salt and pepper and whizz to a thick green purée. Season the mixture, put it into a bowl and cover.

Prepare the fennel by removing any tough leaves or pieces of stem, but leaving enough of the stem to hold the leaves together at the base. Cut each down first into halves, then into quarters and eighths, so that they are still joined together at the base if possible. Steam or parboil the fennel for about 8 minutes, or until it is just tender without being at all soggy. Drain well and dry with kitchen paper. Brush both fennel with oil and sprinkle with some salt and pepper, then grill them until they are lightly charred on both sides: this will take about 15 minutes. Cover until required. Make a simple dressing by putting the vinegar into a screwtop jar with 3 tablespoons olive oil and some salt and pepper and shaking well to mix.

To assemble the dish, spoon some of the pâté on to four individual serving plates, add some black olives, put four pieces of grilled fennel on each plate, and spoon a little dressing on top of the pâté. (Serves 4)

Served with salad, both the stuffed courgette flowers and this recipe make good light meals, in which case they will serve 2–3 people.

Artichokes Stuffed With Lemon Cream

Although these are a bit fiddly to prepare, they're so good that it's worth the effort – and as they're served cold, you can get all the main preparation done well in advance.

4 globe artichokes	1 tbls chopped fresh chives
1 lemon	salt and freshly ground black
125ml/4 fl oz double cream	pepper

First, half-fill two large saucepans with water and put them on the stove to heat. Next, prepare the artichokes by cutting the bases level and removing any damaged lower leaves. For a restaurant-style presentation, you can trim the points off the leaves with kitchen scissors to make them neat; I don't always bother with this. Wash the artichokes well under the cold tap, pulling back the leaves as much as you can, then divide them between the pans of boiling water.

Squeeze the juice from the lemon and reserve 2 tablespoons. Add the rest to the artichokes, dividing it between the pans. Let the artichokes simmer away for about 45 minutes, or until one of the lower leaves pulls off easily. Remove the artichokes from the water and leave them upside down in a colander to drain.

When the artichokes are cool enough to handle, gently pull back all the leaves to reveal the inner, baby leaves which cover the choke; grasp these firmly and pull them out then, with a sharp knife, cut out the remaining choke, being careful to get out all the prickly bits without taking away any more of the delicious flesh than you have to. Rinse the inside of the artichokes gently under the tap, pat them dry and leave them until just before you want to serve the starter.

Just before serving make the filling. Put the reserved lemon juice into a bowl and add the cream, chives, and salt and pepper. Stir the mixture gently with a spoon until it thickens to a floppy state, but don't get it too stiff. Put each artichoke on to an individual plate, pull back the leaves and spoon some of the cream mixture into the centre. Serve at once. It's best to eat this dish by pulling off the outer leaves one by one and dipping their bases in the dressing, then eating the artichoke base and the remaining dressing with a knife and fork. (Serves 4)

Artichokes come in various sizes: medium to large sizes are best for this recipe.

Chilled Cucumber Soup

This is a light and refreshing soup to make at the height of summer when cucumbers are good and plentiful. If you haven't any home-made vegetable stock (which can simply be the water saved from cooking tasty vegetables such as leeks or fennel), it's better to use water rather than a stock cube.

1 tbls olive oil
1 onion, peeled and chopped
2 cucumbers
8–10 sprigs of fresh mint
300ml/½ pint vegetable stock
   or water

4–6 tbls cream
salt and freshly ground black
   pepper
a little chopped fresh mint to
   garnish

Heat the olive oil in a large saucepan and put in the onion; cover and cook gently for 10 minutes until tender.

Meanwhile, peel and roughly dice the cucumbers. Add these to the onion, along with the sprigs of mint, cover the pan again and leave over a gentle heat for about 20 minutes, or until the cucumber is very tender and transparent. Liquidize the mixture thoroughly, including the mint sprigs, then return it to the saucepan and stir in the stock or water and cream. Season with salt and freshly ground black pepper and leave the soup to cool, then chill it.

Check the seasoning just before you serve the soup because chilling dulls the flavour of foods, then ladle the soup into chilled bowls and sprinkle a little chopped mint on top of each. (Serves 4)

Summer Bean and Fresh Herb Salad

The cooked beans absorb flavours well making this a fragrant salad, refreshing yet quite satisfying. If you want to cook your own beans rather than using canned ones, you'll need 200g/7oz cannellini, haricot or flageolet beans. Soak them in plenty of cold water for several hours, simmer them in fresh water for about 1 hour (a little more for the first two types, a little less for the flageolets) until the beans are tender, then drain. You can dress the salad while the beans are still hot. Some warm crusty bread or rolls go well with this.

2 x 425g/15 oz cans cannellini or flageolet beans, or a can of each
4 tbls chopped fresh mixed herbs such as chives, chervil, parsley, tarragon, mint or dill

1 tbls red wine vinegar
3 tbls olive oil
salt and freshly ground black pepper
1 small lettuce

Drain the beans and put them into a bowl along with the fresh herbs, wine vinegar, olive oil and some salt and pepper to taste. Mix well, then cover and leave until you're ready to serve the salad. (The longer you can leave it the better, because it will give the flavours a chance to develop and blend.) Meanwhile, wash the lettuce and put the leaves into a polythene bag in the fridge to chill them and make them crisp.

To serve the salad, put one or two lettuce leaves on individual serving plates, stir the bean mixture then spoon some of it in top of the lettuce. (Serves 4–6)

Easy Summer Tomato Soup

This is a soup which really makes the most of summer tomatoes, and it couldn't be easier to make.

2 tbls olive oil
1 onion, peeled and chopped
1 kg/2¼ lb tomatoes

salt and freshly ground black
   pepper
a little milk or single cream
   (optional)
fresh basil

Heat the oil in a large saucepan, add the onion, and cook, covered, for 5 minutes or so. Meanwhile, wash and chop the tomatoes roughly (there's no need to skin or de-seed them) and add them to the pan, along with a sprinkling of salt. Cover and cook gently for a further 15 minutes, or until the tomatoes have collapsed. Liquidize them thoroughly and pour them though a sieve into the pan. Add 300 ml/½ pint of water, or milk if you prefer, and a tablespoonful or so of single cream if you're using this.

The soup is also very good without any of these embellishments; just add some water to thin it to a nice light consistency, season with salt and freshly ground black pepper, and snip some fresh basil over the top. Chill the soup before serving – or serve it hot if you prefer. (Serves 4)

SUMMER VEGETABLES
AND SALADS

&

Sunshine Ratatouille

4tbls olive oil
450g/1 lb onions, peeled and
   chopped
450g/1 lb red peppers,
   de-seeded and chopped
2 garlic cloves

450g/1 lb aubergines
700g/1½ lb tomatoes
salt and freshly ground black
   pepper
chopped fresh parsley

Heat the oil in a large saucepan and put in the onions and red peppers. Cover and cook, without browning, for 10 minutes. Meanwhile, peel and crush the garlic and cut the aubergines into 1 cm/½ inch dice. Add these to the pan, stir well, cover again and cook gently for a further 10 minutes.

Put the tomatoes into a large bowl, cover with boiling water and leave for 30–60 seconds, or until the skins will slip off; drain and skin. Quarter the tomatoes, then remove and discard the seeds. Chop the flesh and add to the saucepan. Give it another stir, cover and cook for a further 10 minutes, or until all the vegetables are tender. Check the seasoning, adding more salt and a grinding of pepper, and serve with some chopped parsley on top. (Serves 2–4)

This version of ratatouille always works well for me, and it is quick and easy. It's good both hot and cold, as a first course – or as a main course for a light summer meal, which is how I like to serve it, with the salad suggested here.

Green Salad with Shavings of Parmesan

Put 1 tablespoon wine vinegar and 3 tablespoons olive oil into a bowl with a seasoning of salt and pepper. Give them a stir to make a quick dressing, then put some crisp salad greens on top. Some chopped fresh herbs are good too. Just before you want to serve the salad, stir the leaves gently to coat them lightly in the dressing, and add some thin slivers of Parmesan cheese.

Stuffed Courgettes with Fresh Tomato Sauce

These light and summery courgettes are good served with some French beans and perhaps some buttery new potatoes.

4 plump courgettes, each about 125g/4 oz
2 x 150g/5 oz Boursin cheese with garlic and herbs
sprigs of fresh dill to garnish

FOR THE SAUCE
1 tbls olive oil
1 small onion, peeled and finely chopped
900g/2 lb tomatoes
salt and freshly ground black pepper

First make the sauce. Heat the oil in a large saucepan, add the onion and fry for 5 minutes without browning. Meanwhile, quarter the tomatoes and add them to the pan. Cover and cook over a gentle heat for 10–15 minutes, or until the tomatoes have collapsed, then liquidize, sieve and season. Set aside.

Halve the courgettes and cook them in 2.5 cm/1 inch of boiling water in a saucepan until they are just tender: about 3 minutes. Drain them well. Scoop out the seeds with a pointed teaspoon or grapefruit spoon and discard them. Place the courgettes in a shallow casserole or grill pan. Mash the Boursin cheese to soften it a bit, then put some into the cavity of each courgette, dividing it between them and piling them up well. Put the courgettes under a hot grill until they are heated through and the cheese has just started to brown.

Meanwhile, gently reheat the tomato sauce to serve with them. Garnish with the sprigs of dill just before serving. (Serves 4)

Asparagus with Hollandaise Sauce

As far as I'm concerned, this is one of the best treats of the summer. I like to serve lots of asparagus with this buttery sauce as a main course, accompanied by a salad such as the Lettuce Hearts, Lamb's Lettuce and Summer Herbs one, below. A flinty white wine and fresh strawberries would complete the meal.

450g/1 lb asparagus	2 egg yolks
125g/4 oz butter	sea salt
1 tbls lemon juice	

First prepare the asparagus by removing any tough stalk ends, then shaving down the stems a bit with a potato peeler to trim further if necessary. Wash the stems, especially the heads, well. Cook the asparagus in a steamer until it is just tender, 5–10 minutes, or in a pan of boiling water to cover: it will take a little less time. Drain well.

Meanwhile, make the sauce. Cut up the butter roughly, put it into a small saucepan and heat until it has melted and is boiling. While this is happening, put the lemon juice and egg yolks into a food processor or blender with a good pinch of salt and whizz for 1 minute, to make a pale, thick mixture. With the machine running, pour the melted butter in a steady stream into the food processor or blender through the top of the goblet, and whizz for a further 1 minute.

Let the mixture stand for a minute or two, before serving it with the asparagus. (Serves 4)

Salad of Lettuce Hearts, Lamb's Lettuce and Herbs

Pour 1 tablespoon red wine vinegar, a good pinch of salt, a few grindings of pepper and 3 tablespoons olive oil into a dish and mix together. Then put in 2 tablespoons chopped fresh herbs. Wash 2 little gem lettuces and the lamb's lettuce and pat dry, then tear into pieces and put into the bowl. Just before serving, gently turn the leaves in the dressing, and add 25–50g/1–2oz toasted pine nuts.

Lamb's lettuce, or mâche, is available at many greengrocers and supermarkets now, and it's also really easy to grow.

Summer Spaghetti with Tomatoes and Basil

225g/8 oz spaghetti or
  wholewheat noodles
2 tsp olive oil
1 onion, peeled and finely
  chopped
4 tomatoes

sprigs of fresh basil
salt and freshly ground black
  pepper
freshly grated Parmesan cheese
  (optional)

Bring a large saucepan two-thirds full of water to the boil. Put in the pasta, easing it down into the water, and, when the water comes back to the boil, start timing the pasta: if you're using the wholewheat noodles, cover the pan, take it off the heat, then leave it for 5 minutes.

Meanwhile, heat the oil in a medium saucepan, add the onion, cover and cook for 4 minutes. While the onion is cooking, wash the tomatoes and cut them into eighths, then add them to the onion. Stir-fry them, just to heat through really.

Drain the pasta into a colander, then put it back into the warm pan and add the tomato mixture, some torn basil leaves and some salt and freshly ground black pepper to taste. Serve at once, with the Parmesan cheese if you're using it. (Serves 2)

Fennel, Tomato and Black Olive Salad

Put 3 tablespoons olive oil and 1 tablespoon red wine vinegar into a bowl or shallow serving dish, add some salt and pepper and mix together. Wash 2 fennel bulbs and cut off any leafy parts; chop these and add to the oil mixture. If any of the outer layers of the fennel look tough, remove these, then halve the fennel and slice thinly. Wash and slice 4 tomatoes and add the tomato and fennel to the oil mixture, along with 2 tablespoons black olives. Mix gently and leave for at least 30 minutes for the flavours to blend.

I prefer to buy olives from a delicatessen or a shop specialising in mediterranean foods.

Rice Salad with Yellow and Green Courgettes

The combination of yellow and green courgettes – or baby custard pie squash – makes this a pretty, summery salad. It makes a good light lunch if it's served with a salad, such as Fennel, Tomato and Black Olives, above.

75g/2 oz brown rice	1 tbls lemon juice
25g/1 oz wild rice	grated lemon rind
225g/8 oz mixed green and	2 tbls snipped chives
yellow courgettes or baby	1 tbls olive oil
custard pie squash	salt and freshly ground black pepper

Put the brown rice and wild rice into a sieve and wash under the tap, then put them into a heavy-based saucepan with 300 ml/ ½ pint water and bring to the boil. Cover the pan and turn to heat down as low as possible; leave the rice to cook, undisturbed, for 40–45 minutes, until all the water has gone and it is tender.

Meanwhile, wash, trim and slice the courgettes or baby squash. Steam them for a few minutes until they are just tender, then remove them from the heat and cover them with cold water to cool them quickly and preserve the colour. Drain and pat them dry on kitchen paper.

When the rice is cooked, stir it gently with a fork, adding the courgettes or squash, the lemon juice and a little grated rind to taste, the chives, olive oil and a good seasoning of salt and pepper. Serve as soon as possible, while the salad looks bright and glossy. (Serves 2 as a main course, 4 as a side dish)

Tagliatelle of Summer Vegetables

A mixture of summer cabbage, courgettes and carrots is good for this; allow about 700g/1½lb altogether for four people. Shred the cabbage so that it forms long thin strands, then shave long pieces off the sides of the carrots and courgettes and cut these down to form long, thin strips. Bring half a saucepanful of water to the boil, put in first the carrot, and cook for a minute or two until it begins to get tender, then the cabbage; cook for a further minute, then add the courgette strands and cook for just 30–60 seconds.

Drain the vegetables, return them to the pan, add a knob of butter, some salt and freshly ground black pepper and perhaps some chopped fresh summer herbs just before serving.

Summer Vegetable and Herb Burgers

These light summery burgers are good with a crisp leafy or tomato salad; for a more substantial meal, serve them normal burger-style in a light bun. They need to be eaten as soon as they're cooked as they tend to collapse if kept hot under the grill or in the oven. You will need a firmish soft white cheese – fromage frais would be too runny; and ready-grated Parmesan cheese is best for this recipe because of its dryness.

50g/2 oz French beans
50g/2 oz courgette
225g/8 oz curd cheese
2 tbls chopped fresh herbs such as chives, dill, parsley and chervil
50g/2 oz ready-grated Parmesan cheese
freshly ground black pepper

TO COAT AND FRY
6 tbls soft white breadcrumbs
1 tbls ready-grated Parmesan cheese
olive oil

Wash and trim the French beans then cut them into 1 cm/½ inch lengths; wash and trim the courgette and cut into 5 mm/¼ inch dice. Bring 2.5 cm/1 inch of water to the boil in medium saucepan and put in the French beans; boil for 1 minute, then add the courgette and boil for 30 seconds. Drain into a sieve and refresh them under the cold tap, then pat dry on kitchen paper.

Put the curd cheese into a bowl and mix in the chopped herbs, then stir in the vegetables, Parmesan cheese and freshly ground black pepper.

To make the coating, mix together the breadcrumbs and the Parmesan cheese on a piece of greaseproof paper. Divide the curd cheese mixture into four and put them on top of the crumb mixture; form into flat round burgers, rolling them in the crumb mixture so that they are well coated. Chill until just before you want to serve them.

To finish the burgers, heat 2 tablespoons of olive oil in a frying pan – preferably non-stick – and put in the burgers. Fry them for a minute or two until they are crisp and golden brown on one side, then carefully turn them over and fry them until the other side, too, is crisp and golden brown, and the inside has heated through. Serve immediately with salad or in buns. (Makes 4)

For a completely food-combining version of the summer vegetable and herb burgers, replace the white breadcrumbs in the coating with very dry ready-grated Parmesan cheese and fry the burgers carefully to maintain their shape.

Spinach Roulade with Mozzarella and Tomato Filling

A spinach roulade is a classic dish which can be varied by using different fillings. I particularly like this version, which is good either hot or cold.

450g/1 lb fresh spinach	FOR THE FILLING
or 175g/6 oz frozen	2 x 150g/5 oz Mozzarella
15g/½ oz butter	cheese (packed in water)
4 eggs, separated	4 medium tomatoes
salt and freshly ground black pepper	3–4 sprigs of fresh
grated nutmeg	basil
4 tbls ready-grated Parmesan cheese	

Set the oven to 200°C/400°F/Gas Mark 6. Line a 23 × 33 cm/9 × 13 inch Swiss roll tin with non-stick paper, to extend up the sides.

If you're using fresh spinach, wash it three times in sinkfuls of cold water, then put it into a large saucepan and cook over a high heat for 7–10 minutes, or until it is very tender. Keep pushing it down into the pan with a fish slice as it cooks. Cook frozen spinach in a tiny amount of boiling water, just enough to prevent it from sticking to the pan; it takes much the same length of time. In either case, drain the spinach into a colander and press it very well to extract as much water as possible. Put it into a food processor, along with the butter, egg yolks and a seasoning of salt and freshly ground pepper and nutmeg, and whizz it all at top speed to make a smooth, creamy-looking purée.

Whisk the egg whites until they stand in stiff peaks, then gently add the spinach mixture and carefully fold it into the egg whites, incorporating it as well as you can without stirring too hard. Tip the mixture into the tin, level the top gently and sprinkle it with 2 tablespoons of the Parmesan. Bake for 10–12 minutes, until the top is springy.

While the roulade is baking, get ready a piece of non-stick paper to turn it out on to, by sprinkling it with the rest of the Parmesan. Now prepare the filling: drain the Mozzarella and slice thinly; cut the tomatoes into thin rounds and chop the basil.

Take the roulade out of the oven and turn it out on to the non-stick paper. Peel the paper off the roulade, cover with a layer of Mozzarella slices, then a layer of tomato rounds and finally chopped basil and salt and pepper to taste. Roll up the roulade, starting at one of the long ends. Serve it immediately, or put it on a plate, cover with foil and put it into the oven, turned down to 160°C/325°F/Gas Mark 3, for 15 minutes or so. (Serves 4)

Tomatoes Stuffed with Flageolet Beans, with Rice

Using canned flageolet beans makes this a quick and easy dish to make, although you could use dried ones. You would need

100g/3½ oz if you were using dried beans; soak them in water for a few hours, then boil them in plenty of water for 45–60 minutes, or until they are tender. If you cook extra for another time, they'll freeze perfectly in a suitable container.

4 beefsteak tomatoes
salt and freshly ground black
    pepper
1 x 400g/14 oz can flageolet
    beans, drained
2 tbls chopped fresh basil

1 tsp grated lemon rind

FOR THE RICE
225g/8 oz brown rice, preferably
    Basmati
4 tbls chopped fresh parsley and
    chives

First, set the oven to 200°C/400°F/Gas Mark 6, then put the rice into a medium heavy-based saucepan, add a teaspoonful of salt and 600 ml/1 pint of water. Bring to the boil, cover and leave to cook very gently for 30 minutes, or until it's tender and all the water has gone.

Next, prepare the tomatoes. Slice the tops off – the stalks can stay – and scoop out the seeds to make a good cavity for the stuffing. Sprinkle the insides of the tomatoes with salt and pepper. Mix the flageolet beans with the basil and lemon rind and spoon this mixture into the tomatoes; replace the tops. Put the tomatoes in a shallow casserole and bake them for about 20 minutes, or until they are heated right through but not collapsing.

Finish off the rice by adding the fresh herbs and forking them gently through the rice, fluffing it at the same time. Serve the tomatoes with the rice. (Serves 4)

Lettuce and Nasturtium Flower Salad

This is a simple salad of lettuce, tossed in a dressing of 1 table-spoon wine vinegar and 3 tablespoons olive oil, plus some salt and pepper, some snipped chives and, added at the last minute just before serving, some bright nasturtium flowers.

FRUITS, CUPS AND ICES

ℰ

Summer Ice-Cream Cake

We have a number of summer birthdays in my family and this is a favourite birthday 'cake'.

9 egg yolks
225g/8 oz caster sugar
850ml/1½ pints whipping cream
125g/4 oz chocolate, at least
    50% cocoa solids but not a very
    bitter continental one
125g/4 oz strawberries
grated rind of 4 small or 2 large
    oranges

orange food colouring (optional)
1 vanilla pod

TO DECORATE
whipped cream
strawberries
chocolate curls
slivers of orange rind (optional)

This cake consists of three layers of ice cream, chocolate, orange and strawberry, and real vanilla. Of course you could use different flavourings – sieved raspberries, for a raspberry layer, are good. You make one batch of basic ice cream mixture, then divide it into three portions and add the different flavourings, then set it in layers in a cake tin.

To make the basic ice cream, put the egg yolks into a large bowl or the bowl of an electric beater and whisk until thick and creamy. Put all but 1 tablespoon of the sugar into a small saucepan with 6 tablespoons of water and heat very gently until the sugar has dissolved; turn up the heat and let it bubble for a minute or so until it reaches 110°C/225°F on a sugar thermometer or a drop of it on the back of a spoon forms a thread when pulled with a teaspoon. (It reaches this stage very quickly.) Immediately remove the pan from the heat and pour the syrup on to the egg yolks while you whisk them. Continue to whisk for 4–5 minutes until the mixture is cool and very thick and creamy. Whip the cream until it holds its shape, then fold it into the egg yolk mixture. Divide the mixture into three roughly equal portions in separate bowls.

For the first layer, break the chocolate into a bowl set over a pan of simmering water and heat gently until it has melted. Stir the melted chocolate into one lot of ice cream. Pour this into the base of a 20 cm/8 inch deep cake tin and put into the freezer to set, making sure it is standing level.

Hull and dice the strawberries, then put them into a saucepan with the remaining tablespoonful of sugar. Heat gently until the sugar has dissolved and the strawberries are tender: 5–10 minutes. Cool. Add the grated orange rind to the second bowl of ice cream, and intensify the colouring a bit if you like with orange food colouring. Gently fold in the strawberries. If you have room in your freezer, this can go into the freezer for the moment. For the final ice cream, split the vanilla pod and scrape the gooey black seeds out of the skin, using half or all of the pod to taste. Add this vanilla to the final bowl of ice cream and put that, too, into the freezer.

After about 30 minutes, or when the chocolate layer of ice cream has begun to set, gently spoon the orange and strawberry ice cream on top, in an even layer, and put the tin back into the freezer for another 15–30 minutes, or until the orange layer is beginning to get firm. Then scoop the final layer on top, beating it a bit if it has set round the edges. Smooth the top and leave to set completely.

To finish the cake, have ready some whipped cream in a piping bag fitted with a medium shell nozzle. Take the ice-cream cake out of the freezer and run the blade of a knife around the edges, invert the cake on to a suitable plate – give it a shake and the cake should come out. Pipe a little cream around the edges and in the centre, then put the cake back in the freezer and open-freeze it until required. Or decorate it straight away, with strawberries with their stems still attached, chocolate curls and slivers of orange rind, if using. Serve immediately. **(Serves 12)**

Strawberries in Chocolate Cases

You need a good quality plain chocolate for the cases, but not a bitter continental one. The cases need to be made a few hours in advance, to give them time to set, but not overnight as they gradually become dull.

FOR THE CASES
200g/7 oz plain chocolate, at
    least 50% cocoa solids

FOR THE FILLING
225g/8 oz strawberries
about 3 tbls all-fruit cherry and
    redcurrant soft-set fruit spread
    or redcurrant jelly

TO SERVE (OPTIONAL)
raspberry coulis, see below
a few strawberry leaves to
    decorate

First make the chocolate cases which need to be done a few hours in advance. Break the chocolate into a bowl set over a pan of simmering water and heat gently to melt. Have ready some paper cake cases. Using two cases together for firmness, coat the inside quite thickly with melted chocolate. Repeat with all the cases then leave them for 30–60 minutes to set. Give them all another coat of chocolate, making sure it's quite thick around the rim, as this is where it tends to break. Leave them for several hours to firm up, then peel off the paper cases and put the chocolate cases on individual plates.

Hull, wash and slice the strawberries, then put a few in each chocolate case, piling them up attractively. Gently melt the fruit spread or redcurrant jelly and spoon a little on top of the strawberries, being careful not to get the hot jam on the chocolate. Serve with raspberry coulis if you are using this, and decorate with the strawberry leaves. (Serves 6)

To make raspberry coulis, liquidize 500g/1lb fresh or frozen raspberries with 2 tbls water, then sieve. Add caster sugar as necessary to taste.

Rose Petal Creams

300ml/½ pint plain low-fat
  yogurt
300ml/½ pint whipping cream
2–3 tsp rosewater

caster sugar or clear honey
350g/12 oz raspberries
rose petals to decorate

Put the yogurt and cream into a bowl and whisk together until
the mixture is thick. Add the rosewater and a little sugar or clear
honey to taste. Wash the raspberries and pat them dry very
gently with kitchen paper, then sprinkle them with a little caster
sugar to sweeten them as necessary.

Spoon layers of raspberries and the rose cream into six deep
glasses, starting with raspberries, then cream, followed by more
raspberries, and a final layer of cream. Cover and chill until
needed. Scatter some pink rose petals on top before serving.

The petals can be crystallized first by coating them with lightly
beaten egg white, then sprinkling all over with caster sugar and
leaving to dry and crisp up on a rack covered with non-stick
paper. (Serves 4)

The Ultimate Peach Melba

raspberry coulis (see page 70)
6 large, perfect peaches
25–50g/1–2 oz flaked almonds

FOR THE VANILLA ICE CREAM
300ml/½ pint milk

1 vanilla pod
1 egg yolk
100g/3½ oz caster sugar
300ml/½ pint whipping or
double cream

First make the ice cream. Put the milk into a saucepan with the
vanilla pod and bring to the boil. Meanwhile, mix the egg yolk
with the sugar. Pour the boiling milk over the egg yolk mixture,
stir, then return the whole lot to the saucepan. Stir over a gentle
heat for a minute or two until the mixture thickens slightly and
will coat the back of the spoon thinly – don't let it boil. Remove
from the heat immediately and cool. (You can hasten this

process by transferring the mixture to a bowl and standing it in another bowl of cold water.)

Put the cream into a large bowl and whisk until it forms soft peaks, then gradually whisk in the cooled egg yolk mixture. If you have an ice-cream maker, pour the mixture into that and freeze it according to the instructions. If not, pour it into a suitable container to freeze – or freeze it in the bowl, if your freezer is big enough. As it freezes, whisk the mixture every half hour or so if you can, to break up the ice crystals and make a very smooth ice cream. (It's helpful if you freeze the ice cream in the bowl, or in a container which you can whisk it in, to avoid having to keep transferring it from container to bowl.) Once it's frozen, keep it in a covered container in the freezer. Remove it from the freezer 45 minutes before you want to serve it, to allow it to soften up.

Next, make the raspberry coulis according to recipe instructions and set aside until you need it.

Just before you want to serve the pudding, prepare the peaches by putting them into a bowl, pouring boiling water over them and leaving them for 30–60 seconds, or until the skins will slip off. Remove all the skins, halve the peaches and remove the stones. Put two peach halves on each plate, top with a scoop of ice cream, spoon some raspberry coulis over the top and sprinkle with some flaked almonds. Serve at once. (Serves 6)

Traditionally the peaches for this melba should be poached in a sugar syrup but I much prefer to use really perfect, ripe peaches which do not need cooking. It's a wonderful mixture of flavours.

Curd Cheese Summer Pudding

Although many people love summer pudding, it's never done much for me so I wanted to see if I could make a summer's pudding with a difference. I wanted to make an outside of curd cheese, with a luscious filling of red summer fruits but for a long time I couldn't think how to make it so that the curd cheese could drain. Then I hit on the idea of using a round sieve lined with butter muslin. It worked perfectly, resulting in an unconventional summer pudding which we found delectable.

350g/12 oz soft white skim milk
   skim milk cheese
200ml/7 fl oz double cream
3 tbls caster sugar

450g/1 lb mixed red summer fruit
4 tbls all-fruit cherry and
   redcurrant soft-set fruit spread
a few strawberries to decorate

First, line a 16 cm/6½ inch diameter round sieve with a piece of butter muslin and set it over a bowl so that it isn't touching the base. Next, put the soft white cheese and the double cream into a bowl with the caster sugar and whisk until the mixture is stiff but not breaking up. Spoon a good two-thirds of it into the muslin-lined sieve and press it down, so that it forms an even layer.

Wash, hull and slice the fruit as necessary, then mix it with the all-fruit spread to sweeten it. Spoon the mixture into the sieve on top of the curd cheese, then spread the rest of the white cheese mixture evenly over the top. Cover with several layers of kitchen paper, then a plate and a weight, and leave for several hours or overnight. The curd cheese will drip into the bowl and firm up.

To serve the pudding, remove the kitchen paper and invert the sieve over a serving plate. Turn out the pudding, then gently remove the butter muslin. Decorate with some strawberries with their stalks still attached. (Serves 6)

Chocolate Truffle Cake with Cherries in Kirsch

This is a very indulgent but wonderful pudding.

225g/8 oz plain chocolate,
   at least 50% cocoa solids
25g/1 oz butter
300ml/½ pint double cream
900g/2 lb ripe sweet red cherries

4 tbls kirsch
sugar to taste
50g/2 oz plain chocolate, grated
whipping cream to serve

First of all, line a 20 cm/8 inch shallow tin with a circle of non-stick paper. Break the chocolate into a bowl and add the butter; set the bowl over a pan of simmering water and heat gently for a few minutes until the chocolate and butter have melted. Remove from the heat and leave to cool slightly.

Meanwhile, whisk the cream until it will hold a shape but is not too stiff, then gently fold it into the chocolate. Pour this mixture into the tin and smooth the top. Cover and leave to chill and set for several hours. While the cream is chilling, wash and stone the cherries and put them into a bowl with the kirsch and just a little sugar to taste if necessary. Cover and leave until required.

Just before you want to serve the truffle cake, turn it out on to a plate – if you first loosen the edges, then put a plate over it and give it a good shake, it should come out all right. Cover the top with a thick layer of grated chocolate. Serve with the cherries, and some extra softly whipped cream. (Serves 6)

Summer Berries with Sabayon Sauce

4 egg yolks
50g/2 oz caster sugar
2 tbls Cointreau or other orange
  liqueur

150ml/5 fl oz whipping cream,
  whipped
350g/12 oz raspberries, strawberries and a little extra sugar

Put the egg yolks into a bowl set over a pan of simmering water, making sure that the base of the bowl doesn't touch the water. Add the sugar to the yolks and whisk until the mixture is very thick and creamy: this will take at least 10 minutes so it helps if you have an electric hand whisk. Remove the bowl from the heat and leave it to cool, whisking it often. Stir in the Cointreau and gently fold in the cream. Chill until required.

To finish the pudding, wash, hull and slice the fruit as necessary; spoon a pool of the sauce on to four plates, then put the red fruits in the centre and sprinkle with a little caster sugar. (Serves 4)

A classic sabayon sauce makes a delectable accompaniment for summer berries.

SUMMER MENUS

⅋

Menu

A PERFECT SUMMER
LUNCH IN THE
GARDEN FOR FOUR

LITTLE PEA AND MINT CUSTARDS

SUMMER SALAD ROULADE WITH FRESH HERB SAUCE
LITTLE NEW POTATOES BAKED IN A PARCEL
FRENCH BEAN VINAIGRETTE

JELLIED TERRINE OF RED SUMMER FRUITS
ORANGE ICE CREAM WITH PISTACHIO NUTS

Up To One Week In Advance
❏ Make the Orange and Pistachio Ice Cream.

Up To One Day Before
❏ Make the Little Pea and Mint Custards, the Jellied Red Fruit Terrine, the Fresh Herb Sauce and the French Bean Vinaigrette, cover and keep in the fridge.

1–2 Hours Before
❏ Make and fill the Roulade if you are going to serve this warm; it can be done 3–4 hours in advance if you are planning to serve it cold. Heat the oven so that it is ready 35 minutes before you want to eat the meal, then prepare and bake the potatoes in their parcel.

Little Pea and Mint Custards

Delicate in texture, flavour and appearance, these little custards are a real treat. I make them in dariole moulds of 150 ml/5 fl oz capacity, but little ramekins or old cups would be an alternative.

225g/8 oz shelled fresh peas
butter and ready-grated Parmesan
   cheese for preparing the moulds
sprigs of fresh mint
2 eggs

2 egg yolks
150ml/5 fl oz single cream
50ml/2 fl oz double cream
salt and freshly ground black
   pepper

Set the oven to 160°C/325°F/Gas Mark 3.

Cook the peas in boiling water for a few minutes until they are tender, then drain. While the peas are cooking, grease four moulds well with butter and sprinkle with the Parmesan cheese.

Put the drained peas into a food processor with 3 good sprigs of mint and whizz to a purée then push the mixture through a sieve into a bowl. Add the eggs, yolks and creams and whisk well. Season with salt and freshly ground black pepper. Pour into the mould, put them into a small roasting tin and pour boiling water around them to come at least halfway up their sides. Bake for about 35 minutes, or until they feel set, and a cocktail stick inserted into the centre of one comes out clean.

Turn them out on to warmed plates, if you want to serve them hot; otherwise let them cool in their moulds. I think they're best just warm. They should come out of the moulds all right if you loosen the edges with a knife then, holding them over a plate, give them a shake. Garnish with mint.

Summer Salad Roulade with Fresh Herb Sauce

This light roulade can be served warm or cold; it's good either way.

butter for greasing and ready-grated Parmesan cheese for coating
50g/2 oz curd cheese
4 eggs, separated
150ml/5 fl oz single cream
200g/7 oz Gruyère cheese, grated

salt and freshly ground black pepper

FOR THE FILLING
2 heaped tbls mayonnaise
3 floppy lettuce leaves
2 tomatoes, skinned
2 spring onions, finely chopped

Set the oven to 200°C/400°F/Gas Mark 6. Line a 32 × 23 cm/13 × 9 inch Swiss roll tin with a piece of non-stick paper – it needn't be too tidy. Grease the paper and sprinkle with the grated Parmesan cheese. Put the curd cheese and egg yolks into a large bowl and mix together until smooth, then gradually mix in the cream; finally, stir in the grated Gruyère cheese. In another bowl, whisk the egg whites until they're stiff, then fold these into the Gruyère mixture. Season as necessary with salt and pepper.

Pour the mixture into the lined tin, smoothing it gently to the edges and making sure it's even. Bake for 12–15 minutes, until risen and just firm in the centre. Remove from the oven. Have ready a piece of non-stick paper spread out on the work surface and sprinkled with ready-grated Parmesan cheese. Turn the roulade straight out, face-down, on to the non-stick paper.

Cover with a clean, slightly damp tea towel and leave to cool. (It needs to be cool enough not to wilt the salad filling.)

Spread the cooled roulade with the mayonnaise, then put the lettuce leaves on top. Slice the tomatoes very thinly and put these on top of the lettuce, and finally the spring onions and some salt and pepper. Roll up the roulade, starting from one of the long edges – it's easiest to do this if you first make an incision about 1 cm/½ inch from the edge (but don't cut right through) then bend this down to start the rolling process. Use the paper to help you to roll it firmly. Transfer the roulade to a long serving dish and serve with the herb sauce, potatoes and green beans suggested below.

Fresh Herb Sauce

For the herb sauce, stir 300 ml/½ pint plain low-fat yogurt until it's smooth, then mix in 2 tablespoons each of snipped chives and parsley; add salt and freshly ground black pepper to taste.

Little New Potatoes Baked in a Parcel

Based on Elizabeth David's recipe in *French Country Cooking*, this is one of the easiest and most delicious ways to prepare new potatoes. Scrub or scrape 24 very small new potatoes, then put them on to a piece of greaseproof paper with 2 mint leaves, 50g/2oz butter and 2 pinches of salt. Fold the paper over, then fold down the edges so that potatoes are securely sealed. Bake at 190°C/375°F/Gas Mark 5 for 35 minutes.

French Bean Vinaigrette

Top and tail 450–700g/1–1½lb French beans, the thinner the better. Boil them in 2.5 cm/1 inch of water for 3–4 minutes, or steam them for perhaps a minute of two longer, until they have cooked a little but are still quite crisp. Drain them immediately and put them into a bowl with 1 tablespoon wine vinegar, 2 tablespoons olive oil and some salt and pepper. Leave to cool, stirring them from time to time. Serve warm or cold.

Jellied Terrine of Red Summer Fruits

In this glistening red terrine, strawberries are layered with a fruit spread which holds them together and sets them without gelatine. It can be made a few hours in advance and kept very cold until needed, but only turn it out a moment or two before serving. After the first slice has been cut it will collapse, although it will still taste wonderful. I think something sharp goes well with it – crème fraîche or Greek yogurt.

400g/14 oz strawberries
about 500g/18 oz (1½ jars)
  all-fruit cherry and redcurrant
  soft-set fruit spread

redcurrant leaves and summer
  fruits to decorate (optional)

Hull, wash and dry the strawberries, then cut them into thin slices. Melt the soft fruit spread in a saucepan and pour a little into the base of a 450g/1 lb loaf tin, just enough to coat the base by about 3 mm/⅛ inch. Leave it for a minute or two to begin to set, then put a layer of strawberry slices in on top. Pour in a little more of the melted spread, top with more strawberries, and continue in this way until all the strawberries and spread are used up and the tin is full. Leave to cool, then chill thoroughly.

A minute or two before you want to serve the terrine, slip the blade of a knife around the edges and invert the tin on to a serving plate, giving it a shake. Decorate with a few redcurrant leaves and summer fruits, if using. Serve immediately.

Orange Ice Cream with Pistachio Nuts

The flavour of orange goes well with red summer fruits, and this ice cream makes a good accompaniment for the Jellied Terrine of Red Summer Fruits. Pistachio nuts add a pleasant touch of colour and texture to the ice cream, although you could leave them out if you prefer.

2 medium oranges	300ml/½ pint whipping cream
125g/4 oz caster sugar	50g/2 oz shelled pistachio nuts,
4 egg yolks	quite coarsely chopped

Scrub one of the oranges in hot water, then dry it and grate off the rind finely. Squeeze the juice from both the oranges: you should have about 150 ml/5 fl oz. Put the orange juice into a small saucepan with the sugar and heat gently until the sugar has dissolved; then let it boil for about 4 minutes, until the mixture reaches 110°C/225°F on a sugar thermometer or a little of the syrup forms a thread when pulled between your finger and thumb.

Meanwhile, whisk the egg yolks until they are beginning to thicken: it's easiest to do this with an electric whisk if you have one. Pour the orange syrup on top of the egg yolks, whisking at the same time, and continue to whisk for about 5 minutes, until the mixture is thick and pale. Whip the cream until it holds its shape then fold this into the orange mixture, along with the pistachio nuts.

Transfer the mixture to a suitable container and freeze until firm. This ice cream doesn't need stirring as it freezes, but let it stand at room temperature for 30 minutes before you want to eat it to give it a chance to soften up, and give it a stir before serving. Alternatively, do this beforehand and put scoops of ice cream on to a plate, then refreeze so that you can serve it quickly and easily later.

You can get shelled Pistachio nuts at some supermarkets and these are fine for this recipe.

Accompany this lunch with an aromatic or medium-bodied dry white wine such as a Sancerre or Frascati; or try a dry rosé.

Menu

A FAMILY BARBECUE
FOR EIGHT TO TEN

GRILLED AUBERGINE WITH HALOUMI CHEESE
AND TOMATO SAUCE

CHICK-PEA POLENTA WITH TOMATO AND
ONION SALSA
GRILLED FENNEL AND RADICCHIO
WITH GARLIC CREAM
SUMMER LEAF SALAD

FRUIT AND FLOWER COMPÔTE IN
ROSE HIP TEA

Up To Several Hours In Advance
❏ Prepare the Polenta ready for grilling (this can be done a day ahead if convenient). Make the Tomato Sauce, Garlic Cream, Onion Salsa and Fruit and Flower Compôte. Cover them all tightly and keep in the fridge. Wash the salad and put that in a polythene bag in the fridge, too.

One Hour Ahead
❏ Prepare the radicchio, aubergine and Haloumi cheese ready for grilling. Light the barbecue about 40 minutes before you want to start cooking. Dress and toss the salad at the last minute; reheat the Tomato Sauce. Grill the aubergine, Haloumi cheese, polenta, fennel and radicchio on the barbecue.

Grilled Aubergine with Haloumi Cheese, and Tomato Sauce

You can get Haloumi cheese at large supermarkets. You need to read the packets, because some batches are made with animal rennet and some are not. Haloumi cheese keeps for months in the fridge and it also freezes. Its unusual, firm texture makes it excellent for frying, grilling and barbecuing.

2 large aubergines
450g/1 lb Haloumi cheese
olive oil
cherry tomatoes to garnish

FOR THE SAUCE
2 tbls olive oil

2 onions, peeled and sliced
2–4 garlic cloves, crushes
4 thin slices of lemon
2 x 400g/14 oz can tomatoes
chilli powder
salt and freshly ground black
pepper

First make the sauce, which can be done well in advance. Heat the oil in a large saucepan and put in the onions; cover and cook gently for 5 minutes, add the garlic and lemon slices, cover and cook for a further 5 minutes. Put in the tomatoes, together with their liquid, and a good pinch of chilli powder, and cook uncovered for about 10 minutes, until much of the liquid has disappeared. Liquidize the mixture, including the lemon. Taste and add salt and pepper, and more chilli powder, as necessary.

Cut the aubergines into slices just less than 1 cm/½ inch thick, aiming for 16 decent ones. If you like, sprinkle them with salt in a colander and leave for 30 minutes, then rinse under the tap to remove any bitterness, though I have never come across a bitter aubergine. Cut the Haloumi cheese into similar slices.

Oil a baking sheet and heat under a grill, then put slices of aubergine on to this or straight on to a hot oiled barbecue grid and turn them over, so that both surfaces get oiled. Then grill, first on one side and then on the other, until the aubergine is lightly browned. Put the slices on to a warm plate and quickly grill the cheese in the same way (or do the aubergine slices and the cheese slices at the same time if your baking sheet or grid is large). When both sides of the cheese are flecked with brown and the cheese is crisping at the edges, lift the slices off the baking sheet or barbecue grid with a palette knife and put one on each slice of aubergine. Garnish with the cherry tomatoes and serve with the sauce.

Chick-pea Polenta with Tomato and Onion Salsa

Chick-pea flour can be cooked and made into slices in exactly the same way as polenta flour, but I prefer the chick-pea version. These slices can be fried, deep-fried or grilled, and (possibly without the cumin seeds) are enormously popular with kids and teenagers. They make ideal vegetarian barbecue food and I think they're enhanced by a bit of charring and wood-smoke flavours. The kids tend to smother them with tomato ketchup, but I think a simple salsa, made from tomatoes and fresh coriander, goes best with them. You can get chick-pea flour at health shops, Middle Eastern or Indian shops. It may be called Besan or Gram flour.

175g/6 oz chick-pea flour
2 tsp salt
olive oil

1 tbls cumin seeds
slices of lemon

Sieve the chick-pea flour and salt into a medium saucepan and mix to a smooth paste with 600 ml/1 pint of cold water. Put the pan on the heat and stir gently until the mixture comes to the boil and is thick and smooth. Let it cook gently, heaving and bubbling a bit, for about 10 minutes, until it's very thick, and any raw flavour has gone. Turn the mixture out on to a piece of non-stick paper, spreading it to a depth of about 7 mm/⅓ inch or a bit less. Leave it to get cold – or for several hours if you wish – then cut it into rectangles or other shapes. (The shapes can be open-frozen at this point and can later be grilled from frozen.)

Put the shapes on a grill pan or on a barbecue grid that has been greased with olive oil, then turn them, so that they are oiled all over. Sprinkle the cumin seeds on top, then grill the polenta for a few minutes on each side, until they are bubbling, flecked with brown and crisp at the edges. They may seem a bit soft when you turn them, but they'll crisp up as the second side cooks and should prove quite manageable as long as you have a good fish slice to turn them with. Serve with slices of lemon and tomato and onion salsa.

Tomato and Onion Salsa

Fry 1 mild onion, peeled and sliced, gently in a little oil for 7 minutes, until almost tender. Halve, seed and finely chop a green chilli, being careful not to get the juice anywhere near your eyes and to wash your hands afterwards. Add the chilli to the onion and fry for a further 2–3 minutes, them remove from the heat and put the mixture into a bowl.

Skin 900g/2lb of tomatoes by covering them with boiling water, leaving for 60 seconds, then draining and slipping off the skins with a sharp knife. Chop the tomatoes coarsely, discarding any tough bits of stem, and add the tomatoes to the bowl. Pare off one or two strips of skin from a lime and snip them into shreds; squeeze the juice from the lime. Add to the tomatoes, with about 4–6 teaspoons chopped coriander leaves and some salt and pepper.

Grilled Fennel and Radicchio with Garlic Cream

4 fennel bulbs
2 radicchio
olive oil
salt and freshly ground black pepper
lemon slices or fresh herb sprigs
   to garnish

FOR THE GARLIC CREAM
2 x 150g/5 oz Boursin garlic
   and herb cream cheese

The garlic cream can be made in advance and kept in a covered dish in the fridge. To make it, simply mash the garlic cream cheese to break it up and beat in 125 ml/4 fl oz hot water to make a smooth, creamy mixture.

To prepare the vegetables, trim the fennel and radicchio, removing any tough leaves and pieces of stem but leaving enough of the stem to hold the leaves together at the base. Cut each down first into halves, then into quarters and eighths, so that they are still joined together at the base if possible. Steam or parboil the fennel for about 8 minutes, or until it is just tender without being at all soggy. Drain well and dry with kitchen paper.

Brush both the fennel and the radicchio with oil and sprinkle with some salt and pepper, then grill them over hot coals until they are lightly charred on both sides: this will take about 5–8 minutes on a barbecue and slightly longer, about 15 minutes, on a conventional grill. They can be served warm, like a salad, so can be done ahead of the other barbecue items if more convenient. Garnish them with lemon slices and serve them with the garlic cream sauce.

Summer Leaf Salad

This salad is never the same twice, because you can put in whatever leaves and herbs happen to be available. Sometimes I've made it with just garden lettuce and as many different herbs as I could add, but it's more interesting when you use a good variety of leaves. When they're available, I like to put in tender dandelion and nasturtium leaves, baby spinach leaves, rocket, lamb's lettuce and any red, frilly or fancy-leaf lettuce, as well as the basic type.

1 ordinary lettuce or 2 little gem
1 frisée or oak-leaf lettuce
rocket, nasturtium, dandelion,
   and lamb's lettuce leaves, as
   available

FOR THE DRESSING
2 tbls red wine vinegar
6 tbls olive oil
salt and freshly ground black
   pepper
4 tbls chopped fresh herbs such
   as chives, mint, parsley, basil,
   dill, as available

Wash the lettuces and other leaves and shake or spin them dry. Make the dressing straight into the bowl from which you want to serve the salad. Put the vinegar and oil into the bowl with a good seasoning of salt and freshly ground black pepper and mix them until they emulsify; then stir in the chopped herbs.

Put the salad leaves in on top of the dressing, tearing them into manageable sizes as you do so. Toss the salad at the last minute, just before you want to serve it, so that the leaves are all crisp and lightly coated with the herb vinaigrette.

Fruit and Flower Compôte in Rose Hip Tea

The tea gives this compôte an intriguing flavour. Look for tea bags which contain both rosehip and hibiscus; the ones I particularly like are flavoured with raspberry, too; they're called Raspberry Rendezvous, made by the London Herb and Spice Company.

2 x 350g/12 oz all-fruit cherry and redcurrant soft-set fruit spread
6 rosehip, hibiscus and raspberry tea bags

8 ripe nectarines
rose petals and a few small summer flowers such as borage, lavender, pinks

Put the all-fruit spread into a saucepan with 225 ml/8 fl oz water and the tea bags, and heat gently until the spread has melted. Remove from the heat and tip the mixture into a large bowl.

Wash the nectarines, then cut them into thin slices, discarding the stone. Add the slices to the bowl and mix well. Cover and leave for at least an hour for all the flavours to develop.

Just before serving the fruit salad, remove the tea bags, squeezing all the liquid out of them and adding this to the fruit salad. Serve the compôte in a shallow glass bowl with the petals and flowers scattered on top.

Blackberry Fool

The sweeter the blackberries are the better, because you'll need to add less sugar.

450g/1 lb blackberries
1–2 tbls all-fruit cherry and redcurrant soft-set spread

150ml/5 fl oz plain yogurt
150ml/5 fl oz whipping cream
sugar to taste

Wash the blackberries, then put them into a saucepan with the fruit spread and cook over a gentle heat for a few minutes until the juices run and the blackberries are very tender. Purée the blackberries in a food processor, then push this purée through a nylon sieve to remove the seeds.

When the mixture is cool, reserve about two tablespoons of the blackberry mixture and stir the yogurt into the rest, then whisk the cream and fold that into the mixture. Taste and add a little sugar if necessary. Divide the fool between four bowls and spoon the reserved blackberry mixture on top. (Serves 4)

Pimms, for a summery touch, goes well with this menu, or lager, beer or cider for those who prefer these. My personal choice would be a chilled light fruity red such as a Beaujolais.

AUTUMN

&

AUTUMN

℞

The heat of summer gives way to the mellowness of autumn. The days become shorter and the path of the sun gets lower in the sky, crossing the equator at the time of the autumn equinox. The harvest, the precious fruits and vegetables, grains and seeds which will sustain us throughout the darkest months of the year, is gathered in. The life-processes begin to wane, the sap flows less strongly, the leaves become vibrant shades of yellow, gold and red, then drop to the ground as the earth moves to a state of peace and rest. In the country there's the smell of wood smoke in the air, the mornings are misty and cobwebs sparkle in the dew.

During autumn, for me there are three festivals which stand out. First of all, the gathering of the harvest with thanksgiving and celebration; then, later on, Hallowe'en, All Souls and Remembrance Day which to me are linked in that they remind us that there are other dimensions to life apart from the physical. This is a time of year I particularly like, because the world of spirit seems much closer than usual. There is a good astrological reason for this since they all happen during the time when the sun is in Scorpio, the sign which is associated with death, the after-life and the world of spirit. Scorpio is the opposite sign to Taurus, and both signs belong to the fixed element, which accounts for the feeling of underlying peace and stability during this season when in one instance there is the resurgence of life and on the other, the waning: opposite sides of the perpetual cycle of life.

Autumn, like spring, is a time of change, a transition from the heat and sunshine of summer to the cold of winter. Some autumn days can be surprisingly hot, and an Indian summer has its special joy and poignancy; but the breeze has an increasingly cool edge to it. Late summer/early autumn vegetables such as peppers, aubergines, artichokes and fennel bridge the gap between summer and winter admirably, being substantial yet not stodgy; pumpkin, leeks, mushrooms and celeriac also have this quality. All these vegetables are welcome as far as I am concerned, although I have a special affection for pumpkin, with its glorious colour, light texture, delicate flavour and its association with Hallowe'en. As the season advances and we experience the first frosts, heavier, more sustaining foods become available: the first of the autumn root vegetables, the new-season pulses; nuts, with their concentrated nutrients, their warming and protective oils.

As the nights draw in, it seems a natural time to have informal get-togethers, parties and harvest suppers, and welcoming bakes and gratins made from autumn vegetables are an easy and popular way to cater for them; dishes like Aubergine, Tomato and Mozzarella Bake (page 124), Pumpkin and Goat's Cheese Gratin (page 101) and Spaghetti Marrow with Gorgonzola, Cream and Walnuts (page 106). And autumn fruits, especially apples, pears, plums and damsons, plus glowing golden quinces, with their delicate fragrance and flavour, make wonderful seasonal puddings.

Autumn is also the time to hunt for edible treasures in the fields and woods; blackberries, chestnuts, hazel or cob nuts and walnuts on the trees; bilberries and funghi on or near the ground. A mushroom hunt with a couple of reliable guidebooks can be well rewarded, although you need a certain amount of courage to try the results unless you have an expert with you, or can have them expertly identified. Anyway, whether you manage to find any wild mushrooms or just buy them from a shop, having a feast of funghi is one of the delights of the season.

SEASONAL STARTERS

ℬ

Pears in Tarragon Vinaigrette

The success of this simple, refreshing starter depends on using perfect pears, ripe enough to slice with a spoon. I find it best to buy them several days before I need them and let them ripen to the right point. Comice pears give the best result.

3 ripe comice pears
2 tbls tarragon vinegar
2 tbls light olive oil
salt and freshly ground black pepper

several sprigs of fresh tarragon
lollo rosso or red frisée lettuce

Quarter and peel the pears, removing the core, cut them into pieces and put them into a shallow dish.

Put the vinegar, oil and some salt into a jar and shake together until blended, then pour over the pears. Chop the tarragon – there should be 2–3 tablespoonfuls – and add to the pears. Coarsely grind plenty of pepper on top, and stir the mixture gently; if possible leave it for at least 30 minutes for the flavours to develop and blend.

To serve, arrange a few torn leaves of lollo rosso or red frisée lettuce on four plates and spoon the pieces of pear and their juice on top. (Serves 4)

Hot Celeriac Purée on a Bed of Watercress

This was one of those mixtures which happened almost by accident, because of the ingredients I happened to have in, and which turned out to be really good. The combination of hot creamy celeriac purée, cool, crisp, peppery watercress and walnuts is extremely good.

700g/1½ lb celeriac
15g/½ oz butter
2–3 tbls cream
salt and freshly ground black
  pepper

50g/2 oz fresh shelled walnuts
packet or bunch of watercress
1 tbls walnut oil
3 tbls red wine vinegar

Peel the celeriac, then cut it into even-sized chunks. Put them into a saucepan, cover with water, and boil for about 15 minutes, or until the chunks are tender when pierced with a knife. Drain – the water makes a superb stock, I always save it – then mash the celeriac with the butter, cream and salt and pepper to taste.

While the celeriac is cooking, chop the walnuts roughly, then wash the watercress and remove any tough stems. Mix the oil, vinegar and some salt and pepper in a bowl, add the watercress and mix.

To serve, divide the watercress between four plates, put a mound of the celeriac on top and sprinkle with the walnuts. (Serves 4)

Buy walnuts from a shop which has a quick turnover so that they will be really fresh with no hint of bitterness.

Fried Pumpkin Slices with Deep-Fried Sage

Thinly sliced pumpkin, fried in olive oil until it is crisp on the outside, tender within, makes a quick, good starter. The crisp, deep-fried sage makes an attractive garnish, and is quick to do.

a little oil for deep-frying	4 garlic cloves, peeled
12 sprigs of fresh sage	olive oil
600g/1¼ lb pumpkin, weighed with skin and seeds	Maldon salt
	freshly grated Parmesan cheese (optional)

First prepare the deep-fried sage for the garnish. Heat 2.5 cm/ 1 inch of oil in a small saucepan. When it is sizzling hot, put in some of the sage sprigs and deep-fry for a minute or two until they are crunchy, then drain them on kitchen paper and repeat the process with the rest. Keep on one side until required.

Peel the skin from the piece of pumpkin and remove the seeds and threads. Cut the flesh into long slim pieces something like 10 cm/4 inches by 2.5–4 cm/1–1½ inches, and not more than 5 mm/¼ inch thick. Crush the garlic to a paste in some salt. With a knife, smear this garlic paste very thinly on each side of the pumpkin slices to flavour them lightly.

Heat a little olive oil in a frying pan, and fry the pumpkin slices for about 3 minutes on each side, or until they are lightly browned and crisp and feel tender when pierced with the point of a knife. Take them out and drain them on kitchen paper. Serve them as soon as possible on warmed plates, sprinkled with a little crunchy Maldon salt and garnished with the deep-fried sage. Hand round the Parmesan cheese separately if you're serving this. (Serves 4)

Maldon salt is my favourite with its crunchy flakes that you don't need to grind. It can be bought from health shops and large high-class supermarkets.

Fennel a la Grecque

Pleasant either warm or chilled, this is good served with some bread to mop up the juices.

4 fennel bulbs	juice of 1 lemon
2 tbls olive oil	1 x 400g/14 oz can tomatoes
1 tbls coriander seeds	salt and freshly ground black
4 strips of lemon peel	pepper

Trim the fennel, saving any leafy bits. Pare off any chunky root part, and if the outer leaves look tough, either remove them or pare them a bit with a sharp knife, depending on how edible they look. Then cut the fennel down into eighths.

Heat the oil in a heavy-based saucepan and put in the fennel; turn it so that it all gets coated with the oil, then cover the pan and leave it to cook gently while you crush the coriander seeds roughly. A pestle and mortar is best for doing this; otherwise improvise by putting them into a small bowl and crushing them with the end of something like a rolling pin. Add the seeds to the fennel, along with the lemon peel and juice, and stir again.

Chop the tomatoes roughly then add them, and their juice, to the pan. Mix gently, cover and leave to cook gently for 15–20 minutes, or until the fennel is very tender and the tomato is reduced to a glistening crimson sauce. Remove from the heat, season with salt and pepper and leave to cool.

Add the reserved fennel leaves, chopped, just before serving. (Serves 4)

Golden Peppers Stuffed with Cherry Tomatoes

This is a pretty starter – red cherry tomatoes and green basil in golden pepper halves – and it's also easy to do. If you can't get cherry tomatoes, it can also be made successfully with ordinary tomatoes, chopped. It is equally good served as it is, or it can be lightly cooked.

2 golden peppers
225g/8 oz cherry tomatoes
1–2 tbls chopped fresh basil

salt and freshly ground black pepper
olive oil (optional)

If you're planning to cook this starter, set the oven to 200°C/400°F/Gas Mark 6.

Halve the peppers, cutting through the stems and leaving these attached, then put the peppers shiny-side up on a grill pan and grill at full heat until the skin has blistered and begun to char. Move them halfway through the grilling so that all the skin gets done. Cover them with a plate to keep in the steam, and leave until they're cool enough to handle. Slip off the skins with a sharp knife – they'll come off easily – and rinse the peppers under the tap to remove the seeds. Finally, put them, the other way up this time, in a shallow casserole dish.

Skin the tomatoes by covering them with boiling water, leaving them for a few seconds until their skins loosen, then draining them and slipping off the skins. Halve or quarter the tomatoes, depending on their size, and mix them with the basil and some salt and pepper. Spoon this mixture into the pepper halves, dividing it between them. Trickle a little olive oil over each if you wish.

Serve the peppers as they are, or pop them into the oven and bake them for 15–20 minutes. (Serves 4)

Sweet Potatoes with Herb Stuffing

3 medium sweet potatoes, about
   300g/10 oz each
25g/1 oz butter
2 tbls snipped chives

1½ tsp chopped fresh thyme
salt and freshly ground black
   pepper

Set the oven to 200°C/400°F/Gas Mark 6. Wash and prick the sweet potatoes. Place them on a baking sheet and bake for about 1 hours, or until they feel soft when squeezed. Holding them in a cloth, cut them in half horizontally, then scoop out the flesh into a basin with a teaspoon, being careful not to break the skins. Choose four of the best skins and place them in a baking dish, discarding the rest.

Add the butter to the scooped-out sweet potato flesh and mash well, then add the chives, thyme and salt and pepper. Spoon the mixture into the skins, piling them up well, then put them back into the oven for about 15 minutes to heat through.

They can be prepared in advance and heated through just before serving; if heating them through from cold, allow a bit longer: 20–25 minutes. (Serves 4)

WARMING MEALS

ℰ

Pumpkin and Goat's Cheese Gratin

I love the contrast of the sharp flavour of the goat's cheese and the sweet creaminess of the pumpkin in this easy autumn gratin. I like to serve it with the Bitterleaf Salad with Walnut Dressing, next page.

900g/2 lb pumpkin, weighed
  with the skin and seeds
25g/1 oz butter
salt and freshly ground black
  pepper

225g/8 oz firm goat's cheese log
  or logs, cut into thin slices
50g/2 oz fresh Parmesan cheese,
  finely grated

Set the oven to 200°C/400°F/Gas Mark 6.

Cut the skin from the pumpkin and remove the seeds and threads, then cut the flesh into even-sized pieces. Cook the pumpkin in boiling water to cover, or steam it until it is tender, then drain and mash it with the butter. (Keep the cooking water, which makes an excellent stock.) Season the pumpkin purée with salt and pepper and put half of it into a shallow gratin dish.

Cut the goat's cheese into thin slices and put these on top of the pumpkin in the dish, then spoon the rest of the pumpkin on top. Sprinkle with the Parmesan cheese and bake for about 30 minutes, or until the gratin in hot and bubbling and the cheese on top is golden brown. (Serves 4)

Bitterleaf Salad with Walnut Dressing

Put 2 tablespoons light olive oil, 1 tablespoon walnut oil, 1 tablespoon red wine vinegar and salt and pepper into a salad bowl and stir. Wash 2 heads of chicory, a raddicchio and a small red oak-leaf lettuce, separating the leaves. Shake them dry, then tear them into the bowl. Add snipped chives.

Just before you want to serve the salad, toss the leaves so that they all get coated in the dressing, and add about 25–50g/1–2oz chopped walnuts.

Grilled Red Pepper and Aubergine

Allow ½–1 red pepper and ½ medium-large (350g/12oz) aubergine for each person. Quarter the peppers, place them shiny-side up on a grill pan and grill at full heat until the skin has blistered and begun to char all over. Cover them with a plate and leave until they're cool enough to handle. Slip off the skins with a sharp knife and rinse the peppers to remove the seeds. Finally, slice the flesh.

Cut the aubergine into 5 cm/2 inch slices. Brush a little olive oil on a grill pan, put the aubergine slices on this (no need to salt them first) and brush the top surface with olive oil. Grill them until the tops are browned. You'll probably find that the bottoms are browned, too; if not, turn the slices over and do the other sides. The aubergines are done when they're browned on both sides and feel tender when pierced with a knife. Blot off any excess oil and serve them with the red pepper.

Lentils and Coriander with Yogurt Sauce

I use canned green lentils for this because they're so quick, although you could use dried ones if you preferred. If you do use dried lentils, you would need 100g/3½oz; just boil them in plenty of water for 45–60 minutes, or until they are tender – there's no need to soak them first, although if you do it will make the cooking time a bit shorter. And if you cook extra, for another time, they'll freeze perfectly in a suitable container. Serve with the Grilled Red Pepper and Aubergine dish on page 102 and a tossed green salad.

2 tsp olive oil
1 onion, peeled and sliced
2 tsp ground coriander
1 x 425g/15 oz can green
  lentils, drained
2 tbls chopped fresh coriander
  leaves

FOR THE SAUCE
1 small garlic clove, crushed
150ml/5 fl oz plain low-fat
  yogurt
salt and freshly ground black
  pepper

Heat the oil in a medium saucepan then put in the onion, cover and cook for 10 minutes, or until it is tender. Stir in the ground coriander and cook for a further 2 minutes. Add the drained lentils, stir gently, and cook for a few minutes until they're heated through. Then add the fresh coriander.

Meanwhile, make a quick sauce by stirring the garlic into the yogurt and seasoning with salt and pepper. Serve the lentils and sauce garnished with the grilled pepper and aubergine slices. (Serves 2)

If you can't get fresh coriander, use parsley – preferably flat-leaf if you can get it.

Spicy Chick Peas with Yogurt and Paprika Sauce

This is very quick, cheap, healthy and easy. I like it just as it is, but for a more substantial meal you can add some good bread – ciabatta or a Middle Eastern bread would be pleasant – or some cooked brown rice with some chopped herbs mixed into it.

2 x 425g/15oz cans chick peas
6–8 plum tomatoes
8 sprigs of flat-leaf parsley
1 tbls olive oil
1 tsp cumin seeds
salt and freshly ground black
  pepper

FOR THE SAUCE
150ml/5 fl oz plain low-fat
  yogurt
small garlic clove, crushed
  (optional)
½ tsp paprika pepper

First make the sauce: mix together the yogurt and garlic, if you're using this, season to taste and leave on one side.

Drain the chick peas; wash and slice the tomatoes, wash the flat-leaf parsley and remove the leaves from the stems. Heat the oil in a large saucepan and add the cumin. Fry it for about 1 minute, until the seeds start to pop, then put in the tomatoes and chick peas. Stir over the heat for 2–3 minutes, until everything is heated through, then add the parsley and season to taste.

Serve the mixture on warm plates, pour on some of the sauce, and sprinkle the sauce with paprika. Or you can serve the sauce separately in a bowl, with the paprika sprinkled on top. (Serves 4)

Spaghetti with Spicy Tomato and Red Pepper Sauce

This quantity of sauce is right for two people or three at a pinch. If you're using wholewheat pasta, 75g/3oz per person will probably be enough, as it's more filling; otherwise allow 125g/4oz per person.

175–225g/6–8 oz spaghetti
olive oil
salt and freshly ground black
  pepper

FOR THE SAUCE
1 tbls olive oil

1 onion, peeled and chopped
1 red pepper
1 garlic clove, crushed
1 x 400g/14 oz can tomatoes
  in juice
1 dried red chilli,
  crumbled

First get the sauce started. Heat the oil in a medium saucepan and put in the onion; cover and cook gently for a few minutes while you wash, de-seed and chop the red pepper. Add this to the pan, along with the garlic, and cook for a further 5 minutes with a lid on the pan. Put in the tomatoes, together with their juice, and the red chilli. Mash the tomatoes a bit with a wooden spoon to make sure everything is well mixed, then cover and cook for about 15–20 minutes, or until all the vegetables are tender and the sauce is thick. Give the sauce a stir from time to time to make sure it isn't sticking.

Meanwhile, fill a large saucepan two-thirds full with water and heat it for the pasta. When the water is boiling, a few minutes before the sauce is ready, put the pasta into the water; give it a quick stir, let it come back to the boil and leave it to bubble away, uncovered, for about 8 minutes, or whatever it says on the packet.

Drain the pasta, then tip it back into the warm pan and add a little olive oil and some salt and pepper. Serve immediately, with the sauce. (Serves 2)

Spaghetti Marrow with Gorgonzola, Cream, and Walnuts

Almost any salad goes well with this – the Chicory, Frisée and Watercress Salad given on page 107 is a particular favourite.

2 x 900g/2 lb spaghetti squash	salt and freshly ground black
25g/1 oz butter	pepper
150ml/5 fl oz double cream	50g/2 oz walnuts, roughly
125g/4 oz Gorgonzola cheese,	chopped
grated	freshly grated Parmesan cheese

Bring to the boil two large saucepans of water: each pan should be big enough to hold one of the squash whole. Prick the squash in a few places, then put one in each saucepan, cover and boil for 30 minutes, or until the squash is tender when pierced with a skewer. Drain the squash and, holding them with a cloth, halve them and scoop out the 'spaghetti' into a hot saucepan. Add the butter, cream, Gorgonzola and some salt and pepper to taste. Stir quickly over a gentle heat, just to distribute all the ingredients.

Scatter over the walnuts, sprinkle with Parmesan and serve at once, on warmed plates. (Serves 4–6)

I love those marrows which, when cooked, contain many strands, like spaghetti. You can cook them in many of the ways you'd cook spaghetti, but they're lighter, and if you're food combining and not mixing starchy foods like pasta with proteins such as cheese, they're particularly useful as a pasta-replacement.

Chicory, Frisée and Watercress Salad

Put 1 tablespoon red wine vinegar into a bowl with 3 table-spoons olive oil and some salt and a good grinding of pepper. Wash and dry 2 heads of chicory, ½ frisée lettuce and a packet or bunch of watercress. Tear the chicory and frisée into manageable pieces and put them into the bowl along with the watercress, on top of the dressing. Toss the salad just before you want to serve it.

Cabbage Parcels with Tomato Sauce

For this recipe you need cabbage leaves which are big enough to make into parcels, but tender. Young spring cabbage is ideal, although you'll be left with the heart of the cabbage; shredded and mixed with mayonnaise, yogurt and lemon juice, it makes a good salad. The cabbage parcels can be served on their own and this quantity, I found, was greedily consumed by two people; under more restrained circumstances, they can be served with another vegetable like French beans, and maybe some baby new potatoes, and made to serve four.

1 spring cabbage	225g/8 oz button mushrooms
2 tbls olive oil	175g/6 oz Cheddar cheese,
2 onions, peeled and chopped	grated
1 garlic clove, crushed	50g/2 oz Parmesan cheese,
1 x 400g/14 oz can tomatoes	preferably freshly grated
in juice	
salt and freshly ground black pepper	

Set the oven to 200°C/400°F/Gas Mark 6.

First, half-fill a large saucepan with water and bring to the boil; while it's heating up, remove and discard any very tough leaves from the cabbage, then carefully ease off any that seem reasonably large and tender, aiming for eight. When the water boils, put in the cabbage leaves, pushing them down below water level. Cover and cook for 5 minutes or so, until they are tender but not completely soggy. Drain them in a colander and refresh them under a cold tap. Finally, spread them out on kitchen paper and blot them dry.

While the cabbage is cooking, heat the oil in another pan and add the onions; cover and cook gently for 5 minutes, then add the garlic and cook for a further 5 minutes. After this, put half the onion mixture into another pan and add the tomatoes and their juice, mashing them with a wooden spoon. Let them cook away for about 15 minutes until they form a thick sauce, then whizz them in a food processor and season with salt and pepper. Wash and slice mushrooms and add these to the pan containing the rest of the onion; fry for 3–4 minutes, until the mushrooms are tender, then remove from the heat and add the grated Cheddar cheese. Mix well, and put a bit of this mixture in the centre of each cabbage leaf; fold over the sides, and roll each leaf up into a neat parcel. Put the parcels into a shallow ovenproof dish, pour the tomato sauce over and sprinkle the grated Parmesan over the top in a fairly thick layer. Bake for 25–30 minutes, until it's hot and bubbling, and the top is golden brown and crisp. (Serves 2–4)

As a variation, you could use large spinach or Swiss chard leaves instead of cabbage.

Mexican Chillies Relenos

This recipe can be prepared ready for baking ahead of time, and the best accompaniment, I think, is a simple, plain salad.

8 small green peppers, each about 75g/3 oz
175g/6 oz vegetarian Cheddar cheese, grated

FOR THE SAUCE
2 tbls olive oil

2 onions, peeled and sliced
2–4 garlic cloves, crushed
2 x 400g/14 oz cans tomatoes
chilli powder
salt and freshly ground black pepper

Set the oven to 200°C/400°F/Gas Mark 6.

Grill whole peppers at full heat until the skin has blistered and charred all over, turning the peppers around as necessary. Remove from the heat and leave them until they're cool enough to handle.

While the peppers are grilling, make the sauce. Heat the oil in a large saucepan and put in the onions; cover and cook gently for 5 minutes, add the garlic, cover again, and cook for a further 5 minutes. Put in the tomatoes, together with their liquid, and a good pinch of chilli powder, and cook, uncovered, for about 10 minutes, until much of the liquid has disappeared. Liquidize the mixture, then taste and add salt, pepper, and more chilli powder as necessary.

With your fingers and a sharp knife, slip the skins off the peppers. Make a slit down one side of each pepper and, with kitchen scissors, snip out the main section of seeds – don't worry if some are left, they won't hurt. Next, stuff each pepper with some of the grated cheese. Pour some of the tomato sauce into a shallow casserole dish, put the peppers on top, then pour the rest of the sauce over them. Bake them, uncovered, for about 20 minutes. (Serves 4)

Artichoke Bases Stuffed
with Mushroom Mousse

For this recipe you need some big artichokes, which are usually available in the early autumn. Stuffed with a light mousse of mushrooms they're good either as a starter or, and I prefer them this way, as a main course. Some spinach, quickly steamed until it has wilted rather than cooked, goes well with them.

8 globe artichokes
lemon juice
900g/2 lb mushrooms
50g/2 oz butter
2–3 garlic cloves, crushed
2 tbls double cream
2 tbls chopped fresh parsley,
    preferably flat-leaf

salt and freshly ground black
    pepper
50g/2 oz pine nuts

FOR THE CHIVE AND
LEMON BUTTER
75g/3 oz butter
2 tbls lemon juice
1 tbls snipped chives

First prepare the artichokes by cutting off most of the leaves to reveal the choke, scraping this out, and trimming and tidying the remaining leaf-bases to form a neat shallow cup. Brush the cut surfaces with some lemon juice to preserve their colour, then cook them in a large panful of boiling water for 20–30 minutes, or until the bases are tender when pierced with a sharp knife. Put them upside down in a colander to drain. Meanwhile, wash the mushrooms, then chop them roughly. Melt the butter in a large saucepan, put in the garlic and mushrooms and cook, without a lid, for about 30 minutes, or until the mushrooms are tender and all their liquid has gone.

Set the oven to 200°C/400°F/Gas Mark 6. When the mushrooms are done, put them into a food processor and whizz to a purée. Add the cream, a squeeze of lemon juice, the parsley and some salt and freshly ground black pepper to taste.

Pat the artichoke bases dry with kitchen paper as necessary and put them, cup-side up, in a lightly greased shallow casserole. Spoon the mushroom mixture into them and top each with a teaspoon of pine nuts. Bake them, uncovered, for about

15 minutes, or until they are heated through and the nuts are golden.

While they're cooking, make the chive and lemon butter: melt the butter in a small saucepan, add the lemon juice, chives and a little salt and pepper as necessary. Serve the artichokes on warmed plates, with a pool of the sauce. (Serves 4)

For wilted spinach you need 450–700g/1–1½lb tender spinach leaves, without much in the way of stem, for four people. Put into 6mm/¼ inch of boiling water in a large saucepan, stirring for a few seconds until the leaves have wilted. (You may need to do several batches). Transfer them to a warm dish, add salt, pepper, olive oil or butter.

MUSHROOMS

§

Mushroom 'Caviar'

As well as being good as a starter with some crisp Melba or plain toast, mushroom 'caviar' makes a good topping for canapés. Including some dried mushrooms in the mixture gives it extra flavour.

15g/½ oz dried morels or
  porcini mushrooms
450g/1 lb mushrooms
1 garlic clove, peeled
2–4 tbls chopped fresh parsley
25g/1 oz butter
squeeze of fresh lemon juice

salt and freshly ground black
  pepper

TO SERVE
a little soured cream
paprika pepper
sprigs of flat-leaf parsley
crisp toast triangles

First prepare the dried mushrooms by putting them into a bowl and adding boiling water just to cover them. Leave them to soak for about an hour. Drain the mushrooms, straining the liquid through a fine sieve or a piece of muslin to remove any grit. Reserve the liquid. If you have a food processor, put the dried mushrooms in that, along with the ordinary mushrooms, washed, the garlic and the parsley, and whizz until everything is finely chopped. Without a food processor, chop all these ingredients by hand; get them as fine as you can.

Heat the butter in a large saucepan and put in the chopped ingredients, stir, then cook uncovered for 15–20 minutes, or until any liquid which the mushrooms produce has boiled away.

Pour in the reserved mushroom soaking liquid and a squeeze of lemon juice and cook for a few more minutes until the mixture is dry again. Remove from the heat and season.

Serve hot, warm or cold, on individual plates, with a heaped teaspoonful of soured cream, a sprinkling of paprika and a sprig of flat-leaf parsley on each. Accompany with crisp triangles of toast. (Serves 4)

To make melba toast triangles, toast pieces of bread from a sliced wholewheat loaf as usual then, with a sharp knife, slit each across. Cut these into triangles, and them, untoasted side up, under a hot grill for a minute or two until golden brown and the edges are curling up.

Wild Mushroom Dip

If you've just got a few precious wild mushrooms, this dip makes the most of them, and the addition of some porcini intensifies the flavour.

10g/¼ oz dried mushrooms, porcini or morels	25g/1 oz butter
	225g/8 oz curd cheese
125g/4 oz wild mushrooms	salt and freshly ground black pepper

Put the dried mushrooms into a bowl and add boiling water just to cover them. Leave them to soak for an hour. Drain the mushrooms, straining the liquid through a fine sieve or a piece of muslin, to remove any grit. Reserve the soaking liquid.

Wash the wild mushrooms, chop them with the dried porcini and cook them in the butter for 5 minutes, before adding the reserved soaking liquid. Let the mixture bubble away for 10 minutes or so until practically all the liquid has gone and the mushrooms are tender. Remove them from the heat.

When the mushrooms are cool, beat them into the curd cheese to make a creamy mixture, and season with salt and freshly ground black pepper. Serve with crudités or pitta fingers. (Serves 4)

Oyster Mushroom and Porcini Timbale

Because oyster mushrooms are flat, I thought they would look interesting if I layered them into a loaf tin, then set them in place with a light custard. This timbale is the result and I think it makes a really attractive and unusual main dish, good served with a Red Wine Sauce and some seasonal vegetables like the Braised Celery on page 115.

10g/¼ oz dried mushrooms, porcino or morels
600g/1¼ lb oyster mushrooms
50g/2 oz butter

1 garlic clove, crushed
salt and freshly ground black pepper
2 eggs
150ml/5 fl oz single cream

Set the oven to 160°C/325°F/Gas Mark 3. Line a 450g/1lb loaf tin with a piece of non-stick paper to cover the base and extend up the short sides; grease the other sides. Put the dried mushrooms into a bowl and add boiling water just to cover them. Leave them to soak for an hour. While they are soaking, prepare the oyster mushrooms by washing them then gently squeezing out excess water and patting them dry.

Melt the butter in a large saucepan and add the oyster mushrooms. Let them cook for about 20 minutes, without a lid on the pan, until they are very tender and have absorbed their liquid. Drain the dried mushrooms, straining the liquid through a fine sieve or a piece of muslin to remove any grit; chop the dried mushrooms finely. Add the chopped mushrooms and their liquid to the oyster mushrooms, along with the garlic, and cook for a further few minutes until they are again dry. Take them off the heat and season with salt and pepper.

Arrange the oyster mushrooms in the loaf tin in layers. Whisk together the eggs and cream, then pour this custard into the loaf tin, gently moving the oyster mushrooms with a knife and tipping the tin, to make sure that the custard seeps down between all the layers. Put the loaf tin in a roasting tin of boiling water and bake it for about 40 minutes, or until it is set and golden brown and a skewer inserted into the centre comes out clean. Run a knife around the edges of the timbale to loosen it, then turn it out on to a warmed serving dish.

This timbale cuts well both hot and cold, but you need to use a sharp, serrated knife. (Serves 6)

You can buy porcini in small packets. They're not cheap but they go a long way and the flavour is excellent.

Tomato and Red Wine Sauce

1 onion, peeled and sliced
1 celery stick, chopped
1 garlic clove, crushed
1 tbls olive oil
sprig of fresh thyme

300ml/½ pint red wine
1 x 400g/14 oz can tomatoes
salt and freshly ground black
   pepper
15g/½ oz cold butter

Fry the onion, celery and garlic in the olive oil with the thyme for 10 minutes, browning them slightly, then add the wine and tomatoes. Bring to the boil, then let the sauce bubble away for about 5 minutes, to cook the tomatoes and thicken a bit. Liquidize the sauce, then pour it through a sieve into a saucepan. Season with salt and pepper.

Just before serving the sauce, bring it back to the boil then remove it from the heat and whisk in the butter, a little at a time, to make the sauce look glossy and thicken it a little more.

Braised Celery

First trim off any roots from 2 heads of celery, then cut the stems down to about 15 cm/6 inches from the base. Now take a potato peeler and shave the outside stems of the celery to remove any tough threads. Cut the celery down into quarters and wash them well under the tap.

Heat 2 tablespoons olive oil in a large saucepan, add 1 teaspoon coriander seeds, a bay leaf, 6–8 peppercorns, and the pieces of celery. Turn the celery gently to coat it in the oil, add a sprinkling of salt, then pour in 600 ml/1 pint of water. Bring to the boil, cover and leave to cook gently for 1 hour, or until the celery is very tender. Remove the celery with a perforated spoon, put it into a shallow dish and keep it warm. Boil the remaining liquid hard to reduce it well and pour it over the celery. Sprinkle with some chopped parsley.

Ragout of Wild Mushrooms

This is a dish to make when you've had a really successful mushroom hunt, or feel like a no-expense-spared special autumn meal. Alternatively, you can improvise by using a mixture of oyster, button and shiitake mushrooms instead of the wild ones (see below). Some baby sprouts and early chestnuts, below, go well with this, to make a complete meal.

1 kg/2¼ lb wild mushrooms	lemon juice
75g/3 oz butter	salt and freshly ground black
3 garlic cloves, crushed	pepper
4 tbls double cream	chopped fresh parsley, preferably
	flat-leaf

Wash, trim and slice the mushrooms; pat them dry on kitchen paper. Melt the butter in a large saucepan and put in the mushrooms and garlic. Cook over a moderate heat, uncovered, until they are tender and any liquid that they make has bubbled away. The time varies according to the type of mushroom; it can be as little as 5 minutes, or as long as 20, but if you test the mushrooms with a sharp knife you'll be able to tell when they're tender.

Add the cream, a squeeze of lemon juice and some salt and pepper to season. Get the mixture really hot, sprinkle with parsley then serve at once. (Serves 4)

By wild mushrooms, I mean ceps (called porcini in Italy) or chanterelles (or morels in the spring) if you're lucky enough to get them; or oyster mushrooms or shiitake which are increasingly available from greengrocers and supermarkets.

Baby Sprouts and Early Chestnuts

You'll need 450–700g/1–1½lb sprouts for four people and 225–350g/8–12 oz chestnuts, weighed before skinning. Really baby sprouts can be trimmed and cooked whole, but if they are larger, I think they're better if you cut them in half. The chestnuts need to be prepared in advance. The easiest way to skin them is to put them on a board on their flat side and make a sharp cut from top to bottom. Put them into boiling water, a few at a time, and boil for 3–5 minutes, or until the cut opens. Then take them out and peel off the skins. Once they're skinned, they need to be cooked in fresh water for about 15 minutes, or until they're tender.

Cook the sprouts in 1 cm/½ inch of fast-boiling water with a lid on the pan for 3–5 minutes, or until they're just done. Drain them (save the water as it makes good stock), add the hot cooked chestnuts with a little butter, and season with salt and freshly ground black pepper.

PERFECT PUDDINGS

❧

Apple and Blackberry layer

For this light pudding I like to use the sweetest apples and black-berries I can find, because the sweeter they are, the less additional sugar you need. You could use cooking apples if you prefer, sweetened with sugar or honey; and for a less-rich cream, you could use half whipping cream and half plain yogurt.

1 kg/2¼ lb sweet apples	450g/1 lb blackberries
caster sugar, honey or	300ml/½ pint whipping cream
no-added-sugar apricot jam	25g/1 oz toasted flaked almonds

Peel, core and slice the apples, then put them into a heavy-based saucepan with 2 tablespoons of water. Cover and cook over a gentle heat for 10–15 minutes or until they have collapsed to a purée. Watch that they don't stick towards the end of the cooking time. Remove from the heat, taste the mixture, and add a little sugar, honey or no-added-sugar apricot jam to sweeten as necessary, then leave to get cold.

Wash the blackberries, put them into a saucepan without any water and cook them over a gentle heat for a few minutes until the juices run. Remove from the heat and sweeten as necessary, then leave until cold. (If they release a lot of juice, strain the fruit from the liquid with a slotted spoon.)

To assemble the pudding, first whip the cream until it forms soft peaks. Put a layer of blackberry mixture into a glass bowl, using about half the mixture; then put half the apples in an even layer on top, and spread half the cream over them. Repeat the layers, ending with a layer of cream, and keeping a few berries in reserve to decorate the top of the pudding. Chill until required – it will keep overnight, if covered with cling film and stored in the fridge. Sprinkle the toasted flaked almonds and reserved berries on top just before serving. (Serves 4–6)

Spiced Quince Compôte with Orange Cream

Although this may not look amazing, being rather low-key in its colouring, it tastes good, especially if you serve it with the orange cream.

990g/2 lb quinces	FOR THE ORANGE CREAM
3 cloves	1 orange
½ cinnamon stick	150ml/5 fl oz thick Greek
50g/2 oz dark brown sugar	yogurt or double cream

Cut the quinces into quarters, remove the peel and cores and slice the flesh fairly thinly. Put the slices into a saucepan with the cloves, cinnamon, sugar and enough water to cover: I used 600ml/1 pint. Bring to the boil, then let them simmer until the quince is very tender and the liquid is reduced to a syrupy glaze. Remove from the heat and leave to cool – this compôte is good served warm or cold.

To make the orange cream, first remove a few long strands of peel with an orange zester for decoration, then grate enough peel to produce about a teaspoonful: finally, squeeze the orange. Add the grated peel to the yogurt or cream, along with 1–2 table-spoons of the juice, or enough to give a good flavour. If you're using cream, whisk it gently until it falls in soft peaks. (You can't use whipping cream for this recipe because the orange will prevent it from becoming thick.)

Serve the compôte in individual bowls, either with a spoonful of cream and some slivers of orange peel on top, which I think is prettiest; or, if not everyone wants cream, serve this in a separate small bowl, decorated with the orange peel slivers. (Serves 4)

Pear and Almond Tart

This is an unusual tart in which the base is made of ground almonds instead of pastry, and maple syrup is used for sweetening. Some lightly whipped cream with a dash of amaretto or poire william eau de vie would be the final touch for a special occasion.

700g/1½ lb sweet pears
6 tbls maple syrup
1 vanilla pod

FOR THE TART CASE
200g/7 oz ground almonds

1 tsp baking powder
1 tbls maple syrup
25g/1 oz butter
few drops real almond essence
(optional)

Set the oven to 180°C/350°F/Gas Mark 4. Cut the pears into quarters and remove the peel and cores, then cut the flesh into thin slices. Put them into a heavy-based saucepan with the maple syrup and the vanilla pod and cook gently, uncovered, for about 10 minutes. The pears should be tender and almost transparent, and bathed in a glossy glaze after this time. Allow to cool.

Meanwhile, make the tart case: mix together, by hand or in a food processor, the ground almonds, baking powder, maple syrup, butter and, if you wish to intensify the almond flavour, a few drops of real almond essence. Press the somewhat sticky dough into a 20 cm/8 inch metal flan tin, pushing the mixture up the sides but being careful not to make it too thick. Prick the case all over and bake for 10 minutes, until the tart is crisp and golden brown. Remove from the oven and leave to cool.

Not more than an hour or so before serving the tart, arrange the pear slices on top of the pastry, removing the vanilla pod (rinse, dry and use again). Pour any glossy liquid from the pan over the pears; if it is watery rather than glossy, boil it up for a few minutes to reduce it before using. (Serves 6)

Figs with Mascarpone

If you can get some perfect figs, this is a luscious way to eat them. I think they need a light red-fruit coulis to go with them; one made from raspberries is best if you can get them, otherwise you could use sweet ripe red plums.

raspberry coulis (see page 70)   125g/4 oz mascarpone
8 sweet ripe figs

First, make the coulis, which can be done well in advance – then leave it to get cool.

Just before you want to serve the pudding, pour a small pool of raspberry coulis on to four plates. Stand the figs on a board with their stalk uppermost, and cut them down, through the stalk, into sixths or eighths, keeping them attached at the base. Put a couple of figs on each plate and open out the cut sections like the petals of a flower. Spoon a little mascarpone into the centre of each 'flower', and trickle a little of the raspberry coulis on top. (Serves 4)

AUTUMN MENUS

೮

Menu

HARVEST SUPPER
PARTY FOR EIGHT

PUMPKIN SOUP

AUBERGINE, TOMATO AND MOZZARELLA BAKE
ROASTED RED PEPPERS STUFFED WITH FENNEL
AUTUMN GREEN SALAD WITH TOASTED HAZELNUTS

FRUIT SALAD WITH
SCENTED GERANIUM CREAM
APPLE ALMOND CAKE

———————————————

Countdown

Up To One Day Before

❑ Make the Pumpkin Soup, cover and keep in the fridge. Make the Apple Almond Cake and the filling, but don't assemble. Make the Aubergine, Tomato and Mozzarella Bake ready for baking.

2–3 Hours Before

❑ Make the Fruit Salad, cover; wash the salad and keep in the fridge.

1½ Hours Before

❑ Set the oven to 180°/350°F/Gas Mark 4. Prepare the Peppers and put them into the oven to cook. 30–40 minutes before you want to serve the meal, move the peppers to the coolest part of the oven and turn up the heat to 220°/425°F/Gas Mark 7. Put the Aubergine Bake into the oven. Cover the peppers with foil if they start to brown too much. Split and fill the cake; make the Geranium Cream; gently reheat the soup; finish making the salad.

Pumpkin Soup

Pumpkin makes a beautiful soup, golden and creamy, with a delicate flavour – and it couldn't be easier to prepare.

1.4kg/3 lb pumpkin, weighed with skin and seeds	salt and freshly ground black pepper
50g/2 oz butter	fresh lemon juice
1 large onion, peeled and chopped	TO GARNISH
2 garlic cloves, crushed	fresh chives
2 tbls single cream	flat-leaf parsley

Cut the skin from the pumpkin and remove the seeds and threads, then cut the flesh into even-sized pieces. Heat the butter in a large saucepan and put in the onion. Cook, covered, for 5 minutes, until it is beginning to soften, then add the garlic and pumpkin. Stir, then cover the pan again and cook for a further 5–10 minutes. Add 1.4L/2½ pints water, bring to the boil, then half-cover the pan and let the soup simmer for 30 minutes, or until the pumpkin is very tender.

Liquidize the soup thoroughly, then pour it back into the saucepan, stir in the cream, and season with salt, pepper and a little squeeze of lemon juice to lift the flavour, if necessary.

Reheat and serve into warmed bowls, then snip some chives and parsley over each bowl.

Aubergine, Tomato and Mozzarella Bake

This warming casserole is as delicious to eat as it is easy to make; make sure you've got lots of crusty bread handy to mop up the juices.

2 small-medium aubergines,
    450g/1 lb in all
salt
1 large onion
olive oil
2 x 400g/14 oz cans plum
    tomatoes
1 tsp dried oregano

glass of red wine (optional)
salt and freshly ground black
    pepper
225g/8 oz Mozzarella cheese
    (packed in water)
50g/2 oz fresh Parmesan cheese,
    grated

Set the oven to 220°C/425°F/Gas Mark 7. Cut the aubergine into 6 mm/¼ inch slices, discarding the stalk. Layer the slices into a colander, sprinkling each layer with kitchen salt. Put a plate and a weight on top and leave on the draining board for 10–30 minutes, depending on how rushed you are.

Meanwhile, make a rich tomato sauce. Peel and chop the onion then fry it in 1–2 tablespoons of olive oil for 5 minutes. Peel and crush the garlic and add to the pan, along with the tomatoes and their liquid, the oregano and the red wine if you're using it. Break up the tomatoes a bit with a wooden spoon, then leave the mixture to cook, uncovered, for about 15–20 minutes, or until the liquid has reduced considerably, leaving a thick, purée-like mixture. Stir from time to time. Season the sauce with salt and pepper.

Rinse the aubergines under the cold tap and pat the slices dry with a clean cloth or kitchen paper. Heat 2 tablespoons of olive oil in a frying pan and fry the aubergine slices in a single layer – you'll need to do several batches. After a minute or two turn the slices over, so that they get cooked and lightly browned on both sides. Lift them out on to a plate or baking sheet lined with kitchen paper and fry the next batch. Cut the Mozzarella cheese into slices about 6 mm/¼ inch thick.

To assemble the dish, put a layer of half the aubergine slices into a large, shallow casserole. Pour half the sauce on top and then lay the cheese slices on top of that. Cover with the remaining aubergine slices and the rest of the sauce, then sprinkle the Parmesan cheese on top. Bake for 30–40 minutes, or until the topping has turned golden brown and the mixture is bubbling. Serve at once.

Roasted Red Peppers Stuffed with Fennel

This is a slight adaption of one of Delia Smith's recipes which I like very much. It can be served hot or cold as a first course or accompanying vegetable, and I also like it as a light main course with other vegetables. The red peppers need to be good medium-sized ones, rather square in shape; and the fennel bulbs need to be fairly small so that when cut into eighths two pieces will fit inside the peppers side by side.

2 fennel bulbs	salt and freshly ground black
4 red peppers	pepper
1 x 400g/14 oz can tomatoes	1 tbls coriander seeds
in juice	8 dsp olive oil

Set the oven to 180°C/350°F/Gas Mark 4. Bring 2.5 cm/1 inch of water to the boil in a medium saucepan. Cut the leafy tops off the fennel, trim the root ends and remove a layer of the white part if it looks as if it's tough. Cut the fennel down into quarters, then eighths, keeping them joined at the base. Cook the fennel in the water, with a lid on the pan, for 5–7 minutes, or until it's tender, then drain it. (Keep the water – it makes marvellous stock.)

Halve the peppers, cutting right down through the stalks, remove the seeds and trim the white part inside to make a good cavity. Arrange the peppers in a roasting tin or shallow casserole dish. Chop the tomatoes and divide the mixture between the peppers, adding a little of the juice as necessary. Season with salt and freshly ground black pepper, then place two pieces of fennel side by side inside the peppers and on top of the tomato, with the root-end towards the stem end of the fennel; push them down neatly to fit and season again. Crush the coriander seeds in a pestle with a mortar or with the end of a rolling pin or wooden spoon, and sprinkle them over the top of the fennel. Finally, pour a dessertspoonful of olive oil over the top of each pepper half.

Bake the peppers, uncovered, for about 1 hour, or until they are very tender and beginning to brown. Serve hot or cold.

Autumn Green Salad with Toasted Hazelnuts

When you're working out quantities for a party, one of the strange laws of life is that the more people present, the less salad they'll eat. So, under normal circumstances, I'd expect this salad to serve four salad-lovers, but for a harvest supper with more people (and lots of other food), it will be enough for about eight.

1 tbls hazelnut oil, if available
2 tbls olive oil or 3 tbls if
  you're not using hazelnut oil
1 tbls wine vinegar
salt and freshly ground black
  pepper
2–4 artichoke bases, cooked,
  cooled and sliced, or
  1 avocado, peeled and sliced

½ frisée lettuce
packet or bunch of watercress
1 celery heart
2 tbls snipped fresh chives
50g/2 oz skinned hazelnuts,
  toasted under the grill

Mix the dressing straight into a salad bowl: put in the hazelnut oil, if you're using it, the olive oil, wine vinegar and some salt and freshly ground black pepper and mix together. Add the artichoke hearts or avocado and mix gently. Wash the frisée and watercress, shake them dry, then put them into the bowl, tearing large pieces as necessary. Slice the celery heart finely, and add that to the bowl, too, along with the chives.

Just before you want to serve the salad, turn it gently so that all the leaves get lightly coated with the dressing, and add the chopped nuts.

Fruit Salad with Scented Geranium Cream

Prepare the sugar for the geranium cream for 3–4 days before you want to serve this pudding to give the flavour a chance to develop.

FOR THE FRUIT SALAD
- 450g/1 lb blueberries or bilberries
- 2 x 350g/12 oz all-fruit cherry and redcurrant spread
- 5 sweet russet apples
- 5 sweet pears
- 5 sweet figs

FOR THE CREAM
- 300ml/½ pint whipping cream
- 2–3 scented geranium leaves, lemon or rose scent not mint
- caster sugar
- extra geranium leaves to decorate

The geranium cream is made by sweetening the cream with sugar which has been flavoured with geranium. To make this sugar, bury several scented geranium leaves in a small jar of caster sugar and leave for 3–4 days or longer (like making vanilla sugar).

To make the fruit salad, wash the blueberries or bilberries and take out any damaged ones or stems. Put them into a heavy-based saucepan with the no-added-sugar spread and heat gently until the spread has melted and the fruit juices begin to run. Pour the mixture into a bowl and leave on one side to cool down. Meanwhile, peel, core and thinly slice the apples and pears; wash and slice the figs. Add all these to the fruit mixture in the bowl and stir gently so that everything is distributed. Cover and leave until required.

Just before you want to serve the fruit salad, make the geranium cream. Whisk the cream until it makes soft peaks, then gently stir in a little of the geranium-scented caster sugar to flavour and sweeten. Transfer to a serving bowl. Garnish with a few scented geranium leaves and serve with the fruit salad.

The sweetening for the fruit salad is one I love to use – no-added-sugar cherry and redcurrant spread, the own brand of one of our large supermarket chains. This is delicate in flavour, whereas some of the other no-added-sugar spreads available are rather powerful.

Apple Almond Cake

This autumn cake consists of layers of light, quick-to-make almond-flavoured sponge cake sandwiched together with a thick purée of russet apples with amaretto. You can make both the sponge part and the apple purée a day or two in advance, but do not fill the cake until shortly before you want to eat it if you do. For a really luscious, richer, variation, you could spread each of the layers with whipped cream as well as apple purée.

FOR THE ALMOND SPONGE
175g/6 oz soft butter
175g/6 oz caster sugar
3 eggs
50g/2 oz ground almonds
1 tsp almond essence
175g/6 oz self-raising flour
1½ tsp baking powder
25g/1 oz flaked almonds

FOR THE APPLE FILLING
1kg/2¼ lb russet apples,
   peeled and sliced
3 tbls amaretto liqueur
   (optional)
no-added-sugar apricot jam,
   honey or sugar to taste

Set the oven to 160°C/325°F/Gas Mark 3. Line a deep 20cm/8 inch round cake tin with greaseproof paper. To make the cake, put the butter, sugar, eggs, ground almonds and almond essence into a bowl, or the bowl of a mixer or food processor, then sift the flour and baking powder. Whisk or process for a minute or two until the mixture is smooth and glossy, then add 3 table-spoons of water to make a mixture which is soft enough to drop reluctantly off a spoon. Spoon the mixture into the prepared tin, level the top, sprinkle with the flaked almonds and bake for 1–1¼ hours, until a cocktail stick inserted into the centre comes out clean. Cool for 10 minutes in the tin, then transfer to a wire rack. Remove the paper when the cake is cold.

To make the filling, put the apples into a heavy-based saucepan with 2 tablespoons of water. Cover and cook over a gentle heat for 10–15 minutes or until they have collapsed to a thick purée, stirring the mixture often to prevent it from sticking. Remove from the heat and allow to cool completely, then add the amaretto, if you're using it, and a little no-added-sugar jam, honey or sugar to taste.

Assemble the cake by cutting it across twice, to make three layers. Put the bottom layer on a plate and spread it with half the apple mixture, then put the next piece of sponge on top and press down. Spread with the rest of the apple purée and place the final layer, with the almonds in it, on top.

Any of the following would be good to drink with this supper: cider, an aromatic dry white wine such as Gewurztraminer, a light dry wine such as Muscadet, or a White Burgundy.

&

Menu

HALLOWEEN PARTY
FOR TEN TO TWELVE

MEXICAN BEANFEAST WITH TOMATO, RED PEPPER
AND AVOCADO SALSAS

PUMPKIN, OKRA AND BABY
SWEETCORN CASSEROLE

MAPLE ICE CREAM
CHOCOLATE PECAN BROWNIES

PARTY CIDER CUP

———————————————

Up To One Week Ahead
❑ Make the Maple Ice Cream.

The Day Before
❑ Make the Chocolate Brownies.

Several Hours in Advance
❑ Make the Mexican Beanfeast, the Pumpkin, Okra and Baby Sweetcorn Casserole and the Tomato and Red Pepper Salsas.

One Hour in Advance
❑ Make the Avocado Salsa. Gently re-heat the Mexican Beanfeast and the Pumpkin, Okra and Baby Sweetcorn Casserole. Remove the Ice Cream from the freezer 30 minutes or so before you want to serve it.

Mexican Beanfeast

3 tbls olive oil
1 tbls cumin seeds
450g/1 lb onions, peeled and sliced
1 garlic clove, crushed
1 x 400g/14 oz can borlotti beans

1 x 400g/14 oz can red kidney beans
1 x 400g/14 oz can cannellini beans
1 x 400g/14 oz can black-eyed beans
chopped coriander to garnish

Heat the oil in a large saucepan, then fry the cumin seeds for 30 seconds. Put in the onions and garlic and cook gently for 10 minutes, with a lid on the pan. Drain the beans, reserving the liquid. Add them to the saucepan, stirring very gently over a low heat to mix them all together, and heat them through without mashing them. Add a little of the reserved liquid if they are in danger of sticking.

Sprinkle with the chopped coriander and serve with Tomato, Red Pepper and Avocado Salsas, taco chips and a spoonful of soured cream.

Tomato Salsa

700–900g/1½–2lb
  tomatoes
juice of 1 lemon

4 tbls chopped fresh coriander
  leaves
salt and freshly ground black
  pepper

Skin the tomatoes by covering them with boiling water, leaving for 60 seconds, then draining and slipping off the skins with a sharp knife. Chop the tomatoes coarsely, discarding any tough bits of stem, and put them into a bowl with the lemon juice, chopped coriander and salt and pepper to taste. Serve in a bowl, to accompany the beanfeast.

Red Pepper Salsa

3 large red peppers
3 green chillis
juice of 1 lemon

salt and freshly ground black
  pepper

Cut the red peppers into quarters, then put them shiny-side up on a grill pan, together with the chillis which can remain whole, and grill at full heat until the skin has blistered and begun to char. Move them halfway through the grilling so that all the skin gets done, then cover them with a plate to keep in the steam. Leave until they're cool enough to handle, slip off the skins and rinse the peppers under the tap to remove the seeds. Skin the chillis, too, then halve them and rinse away the seeds.

Put the pieces of pepper and chilli into a liquidizer with the lemon juice and some salt and pepper and whizz to a purée. Check the seasoning, and serve in a small bowl.

Avocado Salsa

1 lime
2 avocados
1 green chilli
1 garlic clove, crushed (optional)

salt and freshly ground black
pepper
paprika pepper

Scrub the lime then, using a potato peeler, peel off a few pieces of
rind and snip or cut them into shreds to make about a tablespoonful. Squeeze the juice from the lime and put it into a bowl.
Remove the peel and stones from the avocados, cut into rough
chunks and put into the bowl with the lime juice. Halve, de-seed
and finely slice the chilli, being careful not to get the juice near your
face or eyes (wash your hands afterwards), and add to the avocado,
along with the garlic if you're using it, and the shreds of lime.

Mash all the ingredients together with a fork, to produce a
mixture which is creamy without being too smooth. Season
with salt and freshly ground black pepper. Spoon the mixture
into a small bowl and garnish with a sprinkling of paprika.

Spiced Pumpkin, Okra and
Baby Sweetcorn Casserole

1lkg/2¼ lb pumpkin, weighed
  with skin and seeds
50g/2 oz butter
2 tbls olive oil
2 large onions, peeled and
  chopped
2 garlic cloves, crushed

1 cinnamon stick
225–350g/8–12 oz okra
225g/8 oz baby sweetcorn
1 x 400g/14 oz can tomatoes
  in juice
salt and freshly ground black
  pepper

Remove the peel, seeds and threads from the pumpkin and cut
the flesh into fairly thin slices. Heat the butter and oil in a large
saucepan and put in the onions; cover and cook for 5 minutes,
then add the garlic, pumpkin and cinnamon stick, broken in
two. Stir well, then cover again and cook for a further 10
minutes.

Wash and trim the okra and sweetcorn, then either cut them into 1 cm/½ inch lengths, or leave them whole, whichever you prefer, and add them to the pan. Chop the tomatoes and add these, too, along with their juice. Season with some salt and pepper, cover and leave the casserole to cook for 20 minutes, or until the vegetables are all tender.

Check the seasoning and transfer the mixture to a warmed casserole dish.

Maple Ice Cream

You don't have to stir this ice cream as it freezes in order to produce a smooth, velvety texture.

3 egg yolks   300ml/1½ pint whipping cream
75ml/3 fl oz maple syrup

Put the egg yolks into a bowl and whisk until they are pale and thick, preferably using an electric whisk. Put the maple syrup into a small saucepan and boil for 2–3 minutes, until the syrup reaches 110°C/225°F on a sugar thermometer or a drop of it will form a thread when pulled between your finger and thumb. Remove from the heat immediately and pour the syrup on to the egg yolks while you whisk them. Continue to whisk for 2–3 minutes, until the mixture is cool and very thick and creamy. Whip the cream until it holds its shape, then fold it into the egg yolk mixture.

Pour the mixture into a plastic container and freeze until firm. Remove from the freezer about 15 minutes before you want to serve the ice cream to allow it to soften up a little, although it shouldn't get rock-solid in any case.

Look out for real maple syrup, not 'maple-flavoured' syrup.

Chocolate Pecan Brownies

Brownies always make a popular treat and are good to serve either as a cake or as a pudding. You can vary the nuts in these: skinned hazelnuts, brazil nuts or walnuts are also good.

300g/10 oz plain chocolate, not too bitter, at least 50% cocoa solids
125g/4 oz butter or margarine
4 eggs

2 tsp vanilla essence
50g/2 oz barbados sugar
½ tsp baking powder
125g/4 oz pecans, roughly chopped

Set the oven to 180°C/350°F/Gas Mark 4. Line a 20 cm/8 inch square tin with a piece of greased grease-proof or non-stick paper. Break the chocolate into pieces, put it into a saucepan with the butter or margarine, and melt gently.

Meanwhile, put the eggs into a bowl with the vanilla and sugar and whisk at high speed in a mixer or with an electric hand-whisk for about 5 minutes, until they are very thick and pale. Whisk in the melted chocolate and stir in the baking powder and pecans. (There's no flour in this recipe, that's intentional!) Pour the mixture into the tin, easing it gently into the corners. Bake for 40 minutes. Cool in the tin, then cut into squares.

Party Cider Cup

You can really make this cider cup to taste, adding more or less soda water and brandy as you prefer. It should be refreshing rather than too alcoholic and is a good thirst-quenching drink.

1 lemon
5cm/2 inch piece of cucumber
1 red-skinned apple
6–8 sprigs of fresh mint

100ml/4 fl oz brandy
2 x 1L/1¾ pints cider
2 x 500ml/1 pint soda water
ice cubes

Slice the lemon and cucumber finely; wash the apple and cut it into chunky pieces about the size of a cherry. Bruise the mint by crushing it a bit with a rolling pin. Put all these ingredients into a bowl or very large jug (or divide the mixture between two), add the brandy, then cover and leave until just before the party.

When you're ready to serve the cup, add the cider and soda water to the bowl or jug(s), stir, add the ice cubes and serve at once.

Accompany this menu with either the party cider cup, or a medium-bodied French red wine such as Côtes du Rhône (domaine bottled).

WINTER

&

WINTER

ஃ

In winter, the sun's cycle reaches its nadir or lowest point; it never rises very high above the horizon, giving us short days and long nights. The earth lies dormant, the trees are bare, allowing us to see their stark and beautiful shapes against the muted browns, silvers and greys of the winter landscape. At the winter solstice, however, the sun starts its journey back towards us and, in the northern hemisphere, we celebrate the birth of the Christ child in the dark manger, linking this with the return of the life-giving force of the sun and with the awakening of the light within our own hearts.

Winter, for me, and I imagine for many other people in the northern hemisphere, falls into two distinct periods: a short one before Christmas and a more extended one afterwards. The time leading up to Christmas is one of excitement, anticipation and preparation. The shops are full of exotic and colourful items; thoughts are on parties, presents and preparations for the big meal of the year, Christmas dinner. I particularly enjoy the challenge of creating a vegetarian Christmas feast – such as the one on pages 166–72 with the Christmas Wreath as its centrepiece – which delights the senses and brings pleasure.

After Christmas we move into the second phase of winter which is longer and more extended, and often much colder. Without the excitement of Christmas to buoy us up, the warm days of spring seem far away. The sun never gets very strong or high in the sky, and we look to the stored sunshine in vegetables from the earth, dried seeds such as pulses, nuts, grains, stored and dried fruits, to give us energy while the earth lies dormant. We want warming food but, after the richness of Christmas eating, many people fancy simpler, filling, more homely bakes and casseroles, such as Golden Roulade of Lentils with Rich Mushroom Gravy (page 150) and Split Pea and Spinach Dhal (page 160).

Conversely, this is also a time when many people think about dieting and losing weight, an aspect of late-twentieth century living which goes totally against the rhythm of the seasons, when all the foods available suggest that this is a time when nature is encouraging us to gain a pound or two as protection against the cold. Constant worry about weight and the misery of being perpetually either on a diet or feeling one ought to be, is one of the sicknesses, I believe, of modern life in the affluent half of the world.

I used to be on this dieting switch-back – and being a cookery writer doesn't help. But I have found that, for me, the answer lies in compatible eating. That is, putting it at its simplest, not mixing concentrated protein foods – eggs, cheese, dairy produce (and, for meat-eaters, meat, fish and poultry) – with concentrated carbohydrates or starches – bread, potatoes, pasta, flour, rice – at the same meal. Vegetables (except for potatoes, sweet potatoes and sweetcorn) go with everything. Food combining is really a subject in itself, perhaps for a future book, but many of the recipes in this book are compatible, and these are listed in a separate index at the end of the book. I've found that by eating compatible foods, yet at the same time having a wide range of possibilities open to me, there's no feeling of being 'on a diet' or of having to count calories; I simply do not get the cravings for certain foods – especially sweet ones and 'fattening' ones – that I used to.

SATISFYING SOUPS

&

White Winter Soup
with Sun-dried Tomato Purée

The sunshine flavour of sun-dried tomatoes turns this simple soup into a winter treat. Puréed sun-dried tomato is available in jars, otherwise sun-dried tomatoes in oil, puréed in a blender, are similar.

225g/8 oz celeriac
225g/8 oz turnips
225g/8 oz leeks, white part only
1 tbls light olive oil
sprig of fresh thyme

4 tbls single cream
salt and freshly ground black pepper
4 tsp sun-dried tomato purée

Peel the celeriac and turnips and cut them into even-sized pieces; trim, wash and slice the leeks. Heat the oil in a large saucepan and put in the vegetables and the thyme. Cook the vegetables, with a lid on the pan, for about 10 minutes, then add 850 ml/1½ pints of water. Bring to the boil, turn down the heat and leave the soup to simmer for about 30 minutes, or until the vegetables are very tender.

Remove the thyme, liquidize a ladleful of the soup with the cream, then add this to the rest of the soup. Season the soup with salt and pepper, reheat gently, and serve into warmed bowls. Top each with a swirl of sun-dried tomato purée. (Serves 4)

For a vegan version of white winter soup, replace the cream with a non-dairy cream which you can buy at some major supermarket chains.

Stilton Soup

If you haven't any good home-made stock (which doesn't have to be made specially if you make a habit of saving the water in which vegetables are cooked, especially tasty ones like celeriac), it's much better to use water rather than a stock cube or powder. The celery, leeks and Stilton in this soup give it a good flavour in any case.

225g/8 oz outside celery sticks
225g/8 oz leeks
850ml/1½ pints good
   vegetable stock or water
125g/4 oz Stilton cheese

salt and freshly ground black
   pepper
squeeze of lemon juice
1–2 tbls cream (optional)
snipped chives or parsley
   to garnish

Scrub the celery and run a potato peeler down each stick to remove any stringy bits; trim and clean the leeks. Chop the celery and leeks and put them into a large saucepan along with the stock or water; cover, bring to the boil and leave to simmer gently for 1 hour, or until the vegetables are very tender.

Put the soup into a food processor and crumble in the cheese, in rough chunks. Whizz to a purée, then pour the mixture back into the saucepan through a sieve, pressing through any lumps of cheese. Season with salt and pepper; add a squeeze of fresh lemon juice to sharpen the flavour slightly if necessary, and stir in the cream if you're using this. Reheat gently, without boiling.

Top each bowlful with some chives or parsley.   (Serves 4)

Cream of Celery Soup

Apart from tasting good, this soup is an excellent way of using the tough outer sticks of celery which always get left and tend to lurk in the back of the fridge waiting to be thrown out.

2 tbls olive oil
2 onions, peeled and chopped
outside sticks of 1 head of
    celery, about 450g/1 lb in all

850ml/1½ pints vegetable
    stock or water
4 tbls cream
salt and freshly ground black
    pepper

Heat the oil in a large saucepan and add the onions. Cover and cook over a gentle heat for 10 minutes, until the onions are soft but not browned.

Meanwhile, scrub the celery and run a potato peeler down each stick to remove any stringy bits. Chop the celery and add it to the onions, stir, cover, and cook for another 5 minutes. Add the stock or water, bring to the boil and leave the soup to cook gently for 1 hour, or until the celery is very tender.

Liquidize the soup and pour it through a sieve back into the saucepan to remove any remaining tough bits of celery. Stir in the cream and salt and pepper to taste and serve hot. (Serves 4)

Middle Eastern Lentil Soup

225g/8 oz split red lentils
2 onions, peeled and chopped
2 celery sticks
1 garlic clove, crushed
1 tsp ground cumin

1 tbls olive oil
2 tsp ground coriander
juice of ½ lemon
salt and freshly ground black
    pepper

This is a quick and simple lentil soup with a topping of onion fried with ground coriander to make it crisp and spicy. Put the lentils into a large saucepan with half the onions and 1 L/1¾ pints of water (or real vegetable stock if you have it). Run a potato peeler down the celery to remove any stringy bits, then chop the celery and add to the pan, along with the garlic and cumin. Bring to the boil, then let the soup simmer gently for about 1 hour, until the celery and lentils are very tender.

While the soup is cooking, fry the rest of the onion in the oil with the coriander for about 10 minutes, or until it is tender but lightly browned and crisp. Liquidize the soup, add the lemon juice, season with salt and pepper, then stir in the fried onion and coriander. Serve at once. (Serves 4)

For a change, the lentil soup can be made with green lentils instead of split orange ones.

Golden Onion Soup with Cheese Topping

25g/1 oz butter
1 tbls oil
900g/2 lb onions, peeled and thickly sliced
2 garlic cloves, crushed

1.2L/3 pints vegetable stock
salt and freshly ground black pepper
lemon juice
125g/4 oz grated Gruyère cheese

Heat the butter and oil in a large saucepan, add the onions and cook, covered, for 25–30 minutes until they're soft and golden, stirring them from time to time to prevent them from sticking. Stir in the garlic and cook for 2–3 minutes longer before adding the stock. Bring to the boil and let the soup simmer, uncovered, for 10–15 minutes. Season with salt and pepper and a dash of fresh lemon juice. Serve into individual bowls and put the cheese on top. (Serves 4–6)

Broccoli and Red Pepper Soup

You can use purple sprouting broccoli, or the larger pieces of broccoli, for this cheering winter soup.

25g/1 oz butter
1 onion, peeled and chopped
450g/1 lb broccoli
1 small red pepper

2–3 tbls cream (optional)
salt and freshly ground black
    pepper

Melt the butter in a large saucepan, put in the onion, cover and cook for 5 minutes. Separate the broccoli florets from the stems, chop both and reserve a cupful for the florets. Put the rest of the broccoli, stems and florets, into the saucepan with the onion, cover and cook for a further 5 minutes, then add 600 ml/ 1 pint of water or vegetable stock. Bring to the boil, cover and simmer for about 15 minutes, or until the broccoli is very tender.

Meanwhile, in another pan, bring 300 ml/½ pint of water to the boil and cook the remaining florets for just a few minutes, until they are tender. Drain the liquid into the soup, put the florets into a colander and refresh under the cold tap so that they keep their bright colour. Also prepare the red pepper. Cut it into quarters and put these, shiny-side up, on a grill pan. Grill them for 10–15 minutes, until the skin has blistered all over and begun to char, turning them as necessary. Remove from the grill, cover them with a plate to keep in the steam, and leave until they're cool enough to handle. Slip off the skins with a sharp knife – they'll come off easily – and rinse under the tap. Cut into dice.

When the soup is done, whizz it to a smooth purée in a food processor or blender and return it to the pan. Adjust the consistency at this stage – add a little more water or some milk if it needs thinning, also the cream, if you're using it, along with the cooked florets and salt and freshly ground black pepper to taste.

Serve the soup in warmed bowls, with a spoonful of diced red pepper on top of each one. (Serves 4)

Cream of Winter Swede Soup with Cinnamon

Although you can make this soup for next to nothing, it tastes surprisingly luxurious with its velvety texture and hint of cinnamon.

25g/1 oz butter
1 onion, peeled and choped
½ cinnamon stick
600g/1¼ lb swede
4 tbls single cream

salt and freshly ground black
    pepper
caramelized onion rings to
    garnish (optional)

Melt the butter in a large saucepan, put in the onion, cover and cook with the cinnamon stick for 10 minutes. Peel the swede and cut it into small dice, then add these to the pan. Stir, cover and cook gently for a further 5 minutes. Add 1.5 L/2½ pints of water and bring to the boil. Simmer for about 20 minutes, or until the swede is very tender.

Remove the cinnamon stick, whizz the soup to a smooth purée in a food processor, then pour it through a sieve back into the saucepan. Stir in the cream and season with salt and freshly ground black pepper. Garnish with caramelized onion rings which are made by frying onion rings in a little olive oil or olive oil and butter for 10–15 minutes, until they are brown and crisp. Drain them on kitchen paper and float a few on top of each bowlful of soup. (Serves 4)

Carrot can be used instead of swede for a change.

WINTER VEGETABLES AND HERBS

⅋

Golden Roulade of Lentils with Sage and Onion Filling

This is really an interesting variation on a lentil loaf; the mixture is spread flat, then rolled up around a tasty filling of caramelized onions and chopped sage, and then baked. It's good served with some cooked purple sprouting broccoli and roast potatoes.

225g/8 oz split red lentils
50g/2 oz butter or margarine
450g/1 lb onions, peeled and
  chopped
2 tbls lemon juice

salt and freshly ground black
  pepper
2 tbls chopped fresh sage
butter or margarine for basting
sprigs of fresh sage to garnish

Set the oven to 200°C/400°F/Gas Mark 6. Put the lentils into a saucepan with 450 ml/¾ pint of water and bring to the boil. Reduce the heat, cover and leave to cook gently for 15–20 minutes, or until the lentils are tender, then beat in half the butter or margarine.

While the lentils are cooking, fry the onions in the remaining butter or margarine for 10–15 minutes, allowing them to brown, then remove from the heat. Add the lemon juice and salt and pepper to taste to the lentils, then spread the mixture out on a piece of non-stick paper to make a rectangle 17 × 28 cm/7 × 11 inches. Spread the onions evenly on top and sprinkle with the chopped sage.

Starting at one of the short ends, carefully roll up the lentil mixture, using the paper to help you. Keeping the roulade on the paper, lift it on to a baking sheet then remove the paper. Brush the surface of the roulade generously with soft butter or margarine, then bake for about 20 minutes, basting it again after 10 minutes, until the roulade is heated through. It should be brown and crisp on top, but be careful not to over-cook it or it will dry out.

Lift it on to a plate, garnish with a few sprigs of leaves of sage and serve at once, with the Rich Mushroom Gravy, below, or Tomato and Red Wine Sauce (see page 115). Roast potatoes and winter vegetables such as leeks and carrots, or sprouts make an excellent accompaniment. (Serves 6)

Dried sage can be used instead of fresh although the colour is not so good, and you'll only need 2 teaspoons.

Rich Mushroom Gravy

2 tbls olive oil
1 onion, peeled and chopped
1 garlic clove, crushed
175g/6 oz mushrooms, washed and chopped
2 tsp cornflour

2–4 tbls soy sauce
1 tsp vegetarian stock powder
½ tsp yeast extract
salt and freshly ground black pepper

Heat the oil in a medium saucepan, put in the onion and cook it, uncovered, for 5 minutes, so that it browns a bit. Add the garlic, some ground black pepper and the mushrooms, and cook for a further 5 minutes, continuing the browning process. Add 600 ml/1 pint of water and bring to the boil. Blend the cornflour with some of the soy sauce, add some of the boiling liquid, then tip the whole lot back into the pan. Add the bouillon powder and yeast extract, then let the mixture simmer gently for about 10 minutes, to thicken and give the flavours a chance to develop. Adjust the seasoning as necessary – you may not need any salt – and serve with the roulade.

Roasted Winter Vegetables
with Horseradish Sauce

Roasting brings out the flavour of winter vegetables in a delightful way. They make an excellent accompanying vegetable, but I like to eat them on their own, as a complete course, with lemon juice squeezed over them, a good sprinkling of crunchy salt flakes and a tangy horseradish sauce. Leave out the garlic if you wish, but when it's cooked, it becomes very mild and almost creamy and it's easy to pop the cooked garlic cloves out of their skins with a knife and fork.

350g/12 oz celeriac
350g/12 oz parsnips
350g/12 oz swede
350g/12 oz red onions
25g/1 oz butter
2 tbls olive oil
1 garlic bulb
lemon wedges (optional)

FOR THE SAUCE
1–2 tsp horseradish relish
150ml/5 fl oz soured cream or
    Greek yogurt
salt and freshly ground black
    pepper

Set the oven to 200°C/400°F/Gas Mark 6. Put a large pan of water on the stove to heat. Peel the celeriac, parsnips and swede, then cut them into chunky pieces. Trim the tops of the onions and peel off the outer skin without removing the root; cut them into quarters, still leaving the root, which will hold them together.

Put the butter and olive oil into a roasting tin and put it into the oven to heat up; meanwhile, put the vegetables into the pan of water and boil them for 5 minutes. Drain the vegetables and put them into the sizzling hot fat and put them into the oven.

Meanwhile, break the garlic into cloves. Add the unpeeled garlic to the vegetables after about 15 minutes, then roast them for a further 15–20 minutes, or until they are golden brown. Serve at once, garnished with lemon wedges, if using, and accompanied by the sauce.

To make the sauce, simply stir the horseradish relish into the soured cream or yogurt and add seasoning to taste. (Serves 2–4)

Vegetable Goulash

The idea behind this recipe was to make a vegetable version of a traditional goulash or, strictly speaking, paprikash (since it contains soured cream), using white root vegetables instead of white meat. It makes a warming yet light winter dish; I like it with buttered kale, and perhaps a baked potato.

900g/2 lb white root vegetables: turnips, kohlrabi, celeriac, parsnips
225g/8 oz onions
25g/1 oz butter

1 tbls mild paprika pepper
½ tsp caraway seeds
salt and freshly ground black pepper
150ml/5 fl oz soured cream

First, prepare the root vegetables by peeling them, then cutting them into even, bite-sized pieces; peel and chop the onions. Melt the butter in a large saucepan, put in the onions, cover and cook gently for 5 minutes, then add the root vegetables, paprika and caraway and stir well. Pour in 100 ml/3½ fl oz water or vegetable stock and add a teaspoonful of salt. Cover tightly and leave over a gentle heat for 45–60 minutes, or until the vegetables are very tender and bathed in a glossy brick-red sauce. Keep an eye on it and add a tablespoonful of water if it looks as if it's sticking. Stir in 2 tablespoons of soured cream, check the seasoning, then serve, with the rest of the soured cream. (Serves 2)

To make buttered kale, allow 125–225g/4–8oz kale for each person. Remove any tough stems, then shred the kale. Bring 2.5 cm/1 inch of water to the boil in a large saucepan, put in the kale, cover and cook for a few minutes, until the kale is just done. Drain, add butter, salt and freshly ground black pepper.

Baby Winter Squash with Sage, Cream and Gruyère

This is based on a recipe in *The Savoury Way*, by Deborah Madison. These baby squash or 'miniature pumpkins' as Deborah Madison calls them, make an excellent, easy meal. They are particularly good with the Frisée and Orange Salad which follows.

4 baby squash (but not the tiny miniature ones with soft skins)	4 sage leaves
salt and freshly ground black pepper	150ml/5 fl oz single cream
	125g/4 oz Gruyère cheese, grated

Set the oven to 180°C/350°F/Gas Mark 4.

Slice the tops off the baby squash and scoop out the seeds. Sprinkle the insides with salt and grind in some pepper. Stand the squash in a casserole, snip a sage leaf into each one, pour in a spoonful of cream and divide the cheese between them, pushing it into the cavities. Replace the squash tops. Bake the squash until they're tender, around 35–45 minutes, but don't let them overcook and burst.

Serve immediately, with the salad. (Serves 4)

Frisée and Orange Salad

For this simple, colourful salad, wash a head of frisée (or endive), shake it dry and put it into a bowl, tearing the leaves roughly as necessary. Then, holding them over the bowl to catch the juice, cut away the peel and pith from 4 oranges – ruby red oranges are lovely in this salad if you can get them – then slice them into thin circles and add them to the bowl. Sprinkle in a little salt and grind in some pepper to taste. The salad can be left at this point, or you can add a tablespoonful or two of olive oil.

Spiced Rice with Leeks and Red Kidney Beans

Serve this with a tomato and green bean vinaigrette.

225g/8 oz brown Basmati rice
1 onion, peeled and sliced
½ tsp cumin seeds
¼ tsp chilli powder
½ tsp turmeric
1 cinnamon stick

3 cloves
700g/1½ lb leeks
1 x 400g/14 oz can red kidney
  beans
1 tsp garam masala
salt and freshly ground black
  pepper

Wash the rice in a sieve under the cold tap until the water runs clear, then put the rice into a heavy-based saucepan with the onion, cumin seeds, chilli powder, turmeric, cinnamon stick, broken in half, and the cloves. Pour in 600 ml/1 pint of boiling water and put over a moderate heat. Bring back to the boil, then put on a tight-fitting lid, lower the heat and leave to cook gently for 15 minutes.

Meanwhile, remove the roots and outer leaves from the leeks, and slit them down the sides so that you can open them up and wash them under the tap. Then cut them into 1 cm/½ inch lengths. After the rice has been cooking for 15 minutes, put the leeks into the pan on top – but don't stir. Cover and leave it to cook for a further 10 minutes, after which put the drained kidney beans into the pan on top of the leeks. Cover and cook for a further 5–10 minutes, until the kidney beans are hot, the leeks tender, the rice cooked and all the water absorbed.

Remove from the heat, sprinkle in the garam masala and season to taste. Fork through gently to mix everything and fluff the rice before serving. (Serves 4)

Some canned beans contain sugar, others do not. I prefer to use ones without sugar. If you would rather use dried beans, soak 100g/3½oz overnight, drain, put into a pan with plenty of water, boil hard for 10 minutes, then leave to simmer for 1–1¼ hours, or until the beans are tender.

Purée of Butter Beans with Rosemary and Baked Onions

This combination is very warming and good even though it's simplicity itself to put together. It makes a complete meal, although you could serve some steamed carrots or wilted spinach, too, for a bit of extra colour and flavour. I generally use canned butter beans to save time – I choose the ones that have been canned in water and salt but without sugar.

8 medium onions, unpeeled
2 x 425g/15 oz cans butter
    beans, or prepared dried
    butter beans
good sprig of fresh rosemary

sea salt, preferably Maldon, and
    freshly ground black pepper
butter
extra chopped fresh rosemary
    to garnish
olive oil

Start by preparing the onions. Wash and dry them, then place them, unpeeled, on a dry baking sheet or in a roasting tin. Bake in a hot oven – 230°C/450°F/Gas Mark 8 – for 30–45 minutes, or until they feel tender when pierced with a sharp knife.

When the onions are almost done, prepare the purée. Put the butter beans into a saucepan (together with their liquid) and heat gently until they are very hot, then drain them but keep the liquid. Mash the butter beans or whizz them to a smooth purée in a food processor, adding enough of the reserved liquid to make a creamy consistency. Add the rosemary – you can whizz this with the butter beans if you're using a food processor, otherwise chop it by hand. It's best to add it a little at a time, as it's quite pungent. Season the butter bean purée with salt and pepper, then reheat it and keep it warm until you're ready.

Put two onions on each plate – you can leave them whole, or break them open – and put some butter, Maldon salt and freshly ground black pepper on each, along with the purée. Just before serving, top the purée with a bit more chopped rosemary and a spoonful of good olive oil. (Serves 4)

To prepare dried butter beans, you need 200g/7oz beans. Cover the beans generously with cold water and leave them to soak for several hours. Rinse and put them into a pan with at least their height again in cold water. Boil hard for 10 minutes, then simmer for 1–1¼ hours, or until they are very tender. They freeze very well.

Curried Root Vegetables with Coriander Raita

Any root vegetables can be used for this warming winter dish: carrots, kohlrabi, celeriac, parsnips, along with some cauliflower and spices. This is one of those dishes that is even better the next day, after the flavours have had a chance to develop thoroughly. Serve simply with the coriander raita or, for a more substantial meal, with some cooked rice.

900g/2 lb mixed root vegetables
4 tbs olive oil
2 onions, peeled and chopped
1 green chilli
walnut-sized piece of fresh
  ginger
4 garlic cloves, crushed
½ tsp turmeric
2 tsp ground coriander
2 tsp ground cumin

1 x 400g/14 oz can tomatoes
1 small cauliflower
1 tsp garam masala
salt and freshly ground black
  pepper

FOR THE RAITA
300ml/½ pint plain low-fat
  yogurt
3–4 tbls chopped fresh coriander
  leaves

Peel the root vegetables and cut them into dice. Heat the oil in a large saucepan, put in the onions, cover and cook for 10 minutes. Halve, de-seed and slice the chilli, being careful to wash your hands afterwards and to keep the juice away from your eyes. Peel and grate the ginger, then add the chilli and ginger to the onions, together with the garlic, turmeric, ground coriander and cumin. Give it a good stir, add the root vegetables and stir again. Cover and let it cook gently for a minute or two while you open the tomatoes and drain and measure the juice. Chop the tomatoes and add them to the pan; make up the juice to 300 ml/10 fl oz, and add that too. Bring it to the boil, then cover and cook for 15–20 minutes, or until the root vegetables are almost tender.

Meanwhile, cut the cauliflower into quite small pieces and add to the pan; stir well, cover and cook for a further 10 minutes or so until the cauliflower is tender. Stir in the garam masala and add salt and pepper to taste.

To make the raita, simply mix together the yogurt and chopped coriander, stir well, then season with salt and pepper. Serve with the curry. (Serves 4)

Cabbage Tagliatelle with Cream Cheese and Mushroom Sauce

In this recipe, spring greens are treated like tagliatelle and served with a creamy sauce, to make a delicious main course. The Tomato and Basil Vinaigrette which follows goes particularly well with it.

450g/1 lb spring greens
125g/4 oz button mushrooms
1 tbls olive oil
75g/3 oz Boursin cream cheese with
  garlic and herbs

salt and freshly ground black
  pepper

Fill a medium-large saucepan with 5 cm/2 inches of water and put on the stove to heat up. Wash the greens, removing any tough stems or damaged leaves, then shred them into fine, long strips, like tagliatelle. When the water boils, put in the greens, cover the pan, and let them cook for 4 minutes or until just done.

Meanwhile, wash and slice the mushrooms and fry them in the olive oil for 3–4 minutes, until they are tender. Drain the greens, put them back in the hot pan with the mushrooms, and stir in the Boursin and a little salt and freshly ground black pepper to taste. Serve immediately. (Serves 2)

Leeks Parmesan

Another very simple dish which tastes really good. I like it as a quick and easy main course, but it also makes an interesting first course baked in little individual ramekins.

450g/1 lb leeks

50g/2 oz Parmesan, freshly grated is best, but you can get away with ready-grated

Set the oven to 200°C/400°F/Gas Mark 6. Trim the roots from the leeks, then cut off any tough-looking green parts. Slit them down the side then wash them under the cold tap, opening up the layers so that you can get out all the grit. Cut the leeks into 2.5 cm/1 inch lengths. Bring 5 cm/2 inches of water to the boil in a medium saucepan, put in the leeks, cover and cook for 7–10 minutes, or until they feel tender when pierced with the point of a sharp knife.

Drain the leeks – keep the liquid as it makes very good stock – and put them into a shallow ovenproof dish. Sprinkle the Parmesan cheese on top so that the leeks are covered, then bake for 20–30 minutes, until the top is golden brown and crisp. Serve at once, from the dish. (Serves 2)

You can also make a good vegan version of this by mixing the leeks with a knob of margarine before putting them in the dish, and by using ground almonds instead of grated Parmesan cheese for the topping.

Tomato and Basil Vinaigrette

For this salad, which I shamelessly make all the year round now that firm tomatoes and fresh basil are available, simply slice 1–2 tomatoes for each person and put them into a bowl. Tear up some fresh basil leaves and add these to the bowl, along with a splash of red wine vinegar, a little olive oil and a seasoning of salt and a grinding of pepper. Mix it all together and serve.

Wholewheat Pasta Twists with Broccoli and Fromage Frais

For a long time I avoided wholewheat pasta, having had some unfortunate experiences with it. However I've recently started experimenting with it again, and I've had some pleasant surprises, this dish being one of them. I find the nutty flavour of the pasta goes really well with the creamy, slightly sharp, sauce. I like to serve this with a tomato and basil salad like one on the previous page.

225g/8 oz wholewheat pasta twists
15g/½ oz butter
salt and freshly ground black pepper

450g/1 lb broccoli
400g/14 oz fromage frais, very low fat or 8% fat

Bring a large pan of water to the boil, then put in the pasta, bring the water back to a fast boil, and cook the pasta for about 8 minutes, or as suggested on the packet, testing it just before the time given. Drain the pasta, return it to the pan and add the butter and salt and pepper to taste.

While the pasta is cooking, prepare the sauce. Bring 2.5 cm/1 inch of water to the boil in a large pan; wash the broccoli and cut into florets, removing tough stems. Put the broccoli into the boiling water, cover and cook for about 3 minutes, or until it is just tender. Drain, then add the fromage frais and salt and pepper to taste. Keep the sauce warm until the pasta is done, but don't let it get near boiling point or the fromage frais may separate.

Serve the pasta out on to warmed serving plates and spoon the sauce on top. (Serves 4)

Split Pea and Spinach Dhal
– with Raita and Chutney

I find this a pleasant combination of flavours and colours just as
it is; but for a more substantial meal you could add some fluffy
cooked brown rice.

225g/8 oz yellow split peas
1 onion, peeled and chopped
1 garlic clove, chopped
1 green chilli
2 tsp cumin seeds
½ tsp turmeric
225g/8 oz tender spinach leaves,
 stalks removed
1 tsp garam masala
squeeze of fresh lemon juice
salt and freshly ground black
 pepper

FOR THE RAITA
½ cucumber
300ml/½ pint plain low-fat
 yogurt

FOR THE CHUTNEY
4 tomatoes
1 small onion, peeled and sliced
1 tbls lemon juice
1–2 tbls chopped fresh
 coriander leaves

Put the split peas into a medium-large saucepan with the onion
and 850 ml/1½ pints of water, the garlic, the whole green chilli,
cumin and turmeric. Bring to the boil, then let it simmer, half-
covered, for about 45 minutes, or until the peas are very tender
and the mixture is thick but not sticking. Put in the spinach and
cook for a further few minutes, until the spinach is tender. Add
the garam masala, lemon juice and salt and pepper to taste.

While the dhal is cooking, prepare the accompaniments. Peel
the cucumber then cut it into small dice. Put these into a bowl
and stir in the yogurt and some salt and pepper. For the chutney,
slice the tomatoes and put them into a bowl with the onion,
lemon juice, chopped coriander and salt and pepper. Stir, then
leave on one side for the flavours to blend. Serve the raita and
chutney with the dhal.

SEASONAL PUDDINGS

❦

Satsuma Syllabub

You can whisk these up in no time for a refreshing end to a meal. They're rich, so serve small portions – wine glasses make ideal containers for them.

4 satsumas
150ml/4 fl oz double cream
15–25g/½–1 oz caster sugar, or
   an apricot no-added-sugar jam
   to taste

TO DECORATE
curls of satsuma skin

Wash two of the satsumas, then grate the zest part of the rind finely into a bowl. Add the cream, stir, cover and leave for at least 30 minutes (or as long as overnight) for the flavours to infuse. Strain the cream though a nylon sieve into another bowl, pressing through as much of the oily rind as you can, to give flavour but to keep the texture of the syllabub smooth. Squeeze the juice from all the satsumas and add to the cream.

Half-whisk the cream, then stir in sugar or no-added-sugar apricot jam to taste. Whisk again, fairly gently to prevent curdling, until the mixture makes soft peaks, then spoon the mixture into small individual serving bowls or glasses.

Cover and chill until ready to serve, but don't make these too far in advance as the mixture may begin to separate after about an hour. Decorate with the satsuma curls before serving. (Serves 4)

Armagnac Parfait

This parfait is a wonderful dessert for a special occasion; as it's rich it freezes to a velvet-smooth texture without any stirring, so you can put it straight into a mould and just turn it out for serving. The better the quality of the armagnac, the better the result. It makes an excellent Christmas pudding.

6 egg yolks

150g/5 oz caster sugar

600ml/1 pint double or
whipping cream

4 tbls armagnac

Put the egg yolks into a bowl and whisk until they are pale and thick, preferably using an electric whisk.

Prepare a syrup by putting the sugar into a medium saucepan with 4 tablespoons of water. Heat gently until the sugar has melted, then let it bubble for a minute or so until a drop of it on the back of the spoon forms a thread when pulled with a teaspoon. (It reaches this stage very quickly.) Immediately remove the pan from the heat and pour the syrup on to the egg yolks while you whisk them. Continue to whisk for 4–5 minutes, until the mixture is cool and very thick and creamy.

Whip the cream until it holds its shape, then fold it into the egg yolk mixture, along with the armagnac. Pour the mixture into a suitable container and freeze until firm. Remove from the freezer about 15 minutes before you want to serve the parfait, and serve in scoops. (Serves 6)

Rich Chocolate Ice Cream

This is very rich and smooth. It's my favourite chocolate ice-cream recipe, and one of my all-time favourite chocolate dishes.

5 tbls cocoa powder	1.2L/2 pints single cream
4 egg yolks	200g/7 oz plain chocolate,
175g/6 oz caster sugar	at least 50% cocoa solids

Put the cocoa into a bowl with the egg yolks and sugar and blend to a smooth paste with some of the single cream. Put the rest of the cream into a saucepan and add the chocolate, broken into pieces. Heat the cream and chocolate over a gentle heat until the chocolate has melted and the mixture just comes to the boil. Pour some of it over the cocoa mixture, mix well, and pour the cocoa mixture back into the saucepan. Heat gently, stirring frequently, until the mixture thickens enough to coat the back of the spoon, but don't let it boil. (This only takes a minute or so.) Take it off the heat and let it cool, stirring from time to time to prevent a skin from forming.

Pour the cool mixture into a polythene container and freeze until it is solid around the edges. Then beat it well and put it back into the freezer until solid. Remove it from the freezer 15 minutes or so before you want to eat it, to give it a chance to soften up a bit. (Serves 8)

Cranberry and Cinnamon Cheesecake

175g/6 oz semi-sweet
  wholewheat biscuits
75g/3 oz butter
1 tsp ground cinnamon
200g/7 oz Philadelphia cream
  cheese
400ml/¾ pint soured cream
1 egg and 1 egg yolk

75g/3 oz caster sugar
1 tbls lemon juice
½ tsp real vanilla essence

FOR THE TOPPING
125g/4 oz cranberries
75g/3 oz sugar

Set the oven to 160°C/325°F/Gas Mark 3.

Put the biscuits on a chopping board and crush them to crumbs with a rolling pin. Melt the butter in a medium saucepan, then mix in the crushed biscuits and cinnamon. Spread the mixture evenly over the base of a 20 cm/8 inch springform cake tin and press it down with a jam jar. Pop this into the oven for 10 minutes while you make the filling.

Put the cream cheese into a bowl and beat until it is smooth, then gradually beat in the soured cream, egg and egg yolk, sugar, lemon juice and vanilla, to make a smooth, fairly liquid mixture. Pour this into the tin on top of the biscuit crumb base and bake for 1–1¼ hours, or until the cheesecake is set, and a skewer inserted into the centre comes out clean. Turn off the oven but leave the cheesecake in there for 1 hour, then cool, and finally, chill it. The cheesecake benefits from several hours of chilling, or overnight.

To make the topping, wash the cranberries and remove any damaged ones. Put them into a saucepan with 1 tablespoon of water and cook gently for about 5 minutes, or until the cranberries are tender but not mushy. Add the sugar and heat gently until the sugar has dissolved. Boil for 1–2 minutes, until the mixture looks quite jammy, then remove from the heat and pour evenly over the top of the cheesecake. (Serves 6–8)

For a lemon and star fruit variation, omit the cinnamon. Add a good teaspoonful of grated lemon rind to the cheese mixture. Instead of cranberries, spread a small carton of soured cream

over the top of the cheesecake after it is cooked, then leave it in
the oven for 1 hour to cool down, as described. Decorate with
star fruit, cut thinly to produce pretty stars.

℘

Menu

CHRISTMAS DINNER
FOR SIX

WATERCRESS AND RED PEPPER WITH MASCARPONE

CHRISTMAS WREATH WITH CRANBERRIES
AND PORCINI SAUCE
CARROTS IN PARSLEY BUTTER
BABY BRUSSELS SPROUTS
COCK'S COMB ROAST POTATOES
CHRISTMAS SALAD WITH TRUFFLE OIL

ARMAGNAC PARFAIT (SEE PAGE 162)

———————————————

Countdown

Up To A Week Before
❑ Make the Armagnac Parfait.

The Day Before
❑ Make the Porcini Sauce and the Vinaigrette for the salad. Prepare the Christmas Wreath ready for baking; prepare the carrots, sprouts and potatoes, ready for cooking. Grill and skin the peppers; wash the watercress and the salad vegetables and store in polythene bags in the fridge.

1½ Hours Before
❑ Set the oven to 160°C/325°F/Gas Mark 5. Parboil the potatoes, heat oil in the oven, and put the potatoes on to cook; put the Christmas Wreath into the oven about 1 hour before the meal. Assemble the Watercress Starter; make the Christmas Salad but don't toss it.

10 Minutes Before
❑ Prepare pans for the carrots and sprouts; gently reheat the sauce. Cook the sprouts and carrots just before you sit down to the meal; drain them, put into warmed serving dishes and keep warm.

Watercress and Red Pepper with Mascarpone

The colours in this dish make it look like Christmas-on-a-plate! If you prepare the pepper in advance, have the watercress washed and the dressing already made in a jar, the dish can be assembled in moments.

2 large red peppers	salt and freshly ground black
packet or bunch of watercress	pepper
6 tbls olive oil	225g/8 oz mascarpone cheese
2 tbls wine vinegar	

First prepare the red peppers. Cut them into quarters, then put them shiny-side up on a grill pan and grill at full heat until the skin has blistered and begun to char. Move them halfway through the grilling so that all the skin gets done. Leave until they're cool enough to handle, then slip off the skins with a sharp knife – they'll come off easily – and rinse the peppers under the tap to remove the seeds. Cut the peppers into long thin strips, put them into a shallow container, cover and keep cool.

Wash and remove stems from the watercress as necessary; put into a polythene bag in the bottom of the fridge until required. Make a quick vinaigrette by putting the oil into a jar with the vinegar, some salt and a grinding of pepper; shake well, then keep until required.

To assemble the dish, put some sprigs of watercress on six small plates and arrange some red peppers on top, dividing it among the plates. Then, using two teaspoons, put heaped teaspoons of mascarpone dotted around on top, about five to a plate. Coarsely grind some black pepper over the mascarpone. Give the vinaigrette a quick shake, then spoon a little over each plate.

Christmas Wreath with Cranberries

A dramatic centrepiece for a Christmas meal, this Christmas wreath goes well with all the traditional trimmings, and slices well both hot and cold. I love the strong taste of Stilton, but Cheddar, goat's cheese or even feta could be used for different flavours, according to your taste; and you can replace the broccoli with celeriac or other vegetables.

700g/1½ lb large leeks
700g/1½ lb broccoli
butter for greasing
250g/9 oz Stilton cheese, grated
150ml/5 fl oz single cream
4 eggs, beaten
3 tbls chopped fresh parsley
6 tsp chopped fresh thyme
salt and freshly ground black pepper

FOR THE CRANBERRIES
225g/8 oz cranberries
2 tbls all-fruit cherry and
  redcurrant soft-set fruit spread
sprigs of flat-leaf parsley and
  rosemary
sugar to taste

Trim the leeks and remove any tough leaves. Slit the sides of the leeks and rinse them thoroughly under the tap, then cook the leeks in a large saucepan of boiling water for about 20 minutes, or until they are very tender. Drain well – the water makes good stock for the sauce – refresh the leeks under the cold tap, and drain well again. Trim any tough stems from the broccoli, then chop it into fairly small pieces. (There should be 450g/1lb after trimming.) Cook the broccoli for about 5 minutes in boiling water until tender, then drain.

Set the oven to 160°C/325°F/Gas Mark 3. Grease a 1.5 L/2½ pint ring mould generously with butter. Lay single leaves of leek down the sides and base of the ring, going right round until it is all covered. Let the ends hang over the edge for the moment, don't cut them. Chop the rest of the leeks finely and mix with the broccoli, Stilton cheese, cream, eggs, parsley, thyme and salt and pepper to taste. Pour the mixture into the mould – it won't quite fill it, to allow the mixture to rise a little during cooking – and fold the overhanging leek leaves over the top. Put the ring into a baking tin and pour boiling water around, to come halfway up the mould. Cover with foil and bake for 1 hour, or until the mould is set.

While the mould is cooking, prepare the cranberries for the decoration and sauce. Wash the cranberries, removing any bad ones. Reserve some for decoration, put the remainder into a saucepan with the fruit spread. Cook gently for about 5 minutes, or until the berries are soft but not mushy. Remove from the heat.

When the mould is done, take it out of the oven and remove the foil. Loosen the edges of the mould, then turn it out on to a large round warm plate. If a small amount of liquid appears in the centre, blot it up with kitchen paper.

Arrange leaves of flat-leaf parsley and a few tiny sprigs of rosemary all round the top, to resemble a Christmas wreath, then arrange a few cranberries on top, at intervals, to resemble holly berries. Add a few cranberries and sprigs of rosemary around the base if you wish. Sweeten the rest of the cranberry mixture to taste as necessary, and serve it in a bowl or jug, to accompany the wreath.

Porcini Sauce

The wine makes this extra rich and tasty, but it is also extremely good without it – simply increase the amount of stock instead.

20g/¾ oz dried porcini
400ml/¾ pint vegetable stock
50g/2 oz butter
300ml/½ pint dry red or white
    wine

1 tbls Madeira wine or brandy
1 tbls double cream
salt and freshly ground black
    pepper

Put the porcini into a saucepan with the stock and bring to the boil; remove from the heat and leave them to soak for at least 1 hour, or even overnight. After this, strain the stock into a bowl through a very fine sieve or a piece of muslin. Chop the porcini finely, by hand or in a food processor.

Melt the butter in a medium saucepan and add the porcini; cook over a gentle heat for 5 minutes, then add the liquid you drained off the porcini, with the wine. Bring to the boil, and let the mixture bubble for several minutes until it is reduced by half. Stir in the Madeira or brandy and the cream, and season. Serve with the Christmas Wreath.

Carrots in Parsley Butter

You can use baby carrots, or larger ones cut into matchsticks, allowing 700g/1½lb for six people. Scrape and cut the carrots as necessary – baby ones will just need washing – then cook them in boiling water to cover for 4–5 minutes, or until they are just tender. Drain, add a knob of butter, 1–2 tablespoons chopped parsley, a squeeze of lemon juice and salt and freshly ground black pepper to taste.

Cocks' Comb Roast Potatoes

Choose about 1kg/2lb 2oz even-sized potatoes and scrub them. Put them in a saucepan, cover with water and parboil for 5 minutes or until they are reasonably tender. With a sharp knife, remove the skins and cut the potatoes in half widthways. Standing each potato on its cut surface in a baking tin, cut slits in the top about 5mm/¼ inch apart.

Melt 50g/2oz butter, brush this all over the potatoes then sprinkle them with salt. Bake these with the Christmas Wreath, putting them at the top of the oven and allowing 1–1¼ hours for them to become golden and crisp.

Baby Brussels Sprouts

If you can get really tiny Brussels sprouts, they can be cooked whole; otherwise, with larger ones, I prefer to cut them in half as I find they do not go soggy this way. Either way, you'll need 700g/1½lb for six people. Trim the sprouts as necessary, then cook in 1 cm/½ inch of fast-boiling water, with a lid on the pan, for 3–5 minutes, or until they're just done. Drain, add a little butter and some salt, freshly ground black pepper and grated nutmeg.

Christmas Salad with Truffle Oil

Some truffle oil (which you can buy at specialist delicatessens) makes this salad extra special. Choose tender salad leaves – ordinary lettuce, plus some lamb's lettuce (mâche) makes a good combination, or a good continental salad bowl mix. Have the leaves washed and ready, stored in a polythene bag in the fridge. Make up a vinaigrette by putting 3 tablespoons truffle oil into a jar with 1 tablespoon red wine vinegar, some salt and a grinding of pepper; shake well, then keep until required.

Just before you want to eat the salad, give the dressing a quick shake, then pour it into a salad bowl; put in the leaves on top of the dressing, toss the salad gently, and serve.

To accompany this menu, choose either a medium- or full-bodied red such as Côtes du Rhône (domaine bottled), Claret or Chianti Classico; or a medium-dry, fruity white such as Bouches-du-Rhône.

§

Menu

WINTER BUFFET
FOR TEN TO TWELVE

A TRIO OF DIPS – ROQUEFORT, GOAT'S CHEESE AND
FRESH HERB

CELERIAC TERRINE WITH RED PEPPER SAUCE
WARM RED CABBAGE AND CHERRY TOMATO SALAD
BROCCOLI AND BRIE BAKE
LITTLE GEM AND WATERCRESS SALD

COMPÔTE OF EXOTIC FRUITS
FRUITS DIPPED IN CHOCOLATE
CHOCOLATE TRUFFLES

MULLED WINE

———————————

———————————

The Day Before

❑ Prepare and bake the Celeriac Terrine; make the Red Pepper Sauce. Prepare the Broccoli and Brie Bake ready for baking, cover well. Make the Chocolate Truffles and the Exotic Fruit Salad.

Several Hours Before

❑ Make the dips; cover and keep in a cool place. Make the Red Cabbage Salad but don't add the tomatoes. Wash the lettuce and watercress, keep in a polythene bag in the fridge; make the dressing. Prepare the Fruits Dipped in Chocolate.

10 Minutes Before

❑ Preheat the oven; 20–30 minutes before you want to eat, put in the Broccoli Bake. Make the Mulled Wine. Finish making the Red Cabbage Salad and the Lettuce Salad.

Roquefort, Goat's Cheese and Fresh Herb Dips

These dips are all simple to make and, I think, particularly good with some crudités, although crisps and tortilla chips are popular with them too.

FOR THE ROQUEFORT DIP
100g/3½ oz Roquefort cheese
100g/3½ oz fromage frais

FOR THE GOAT'S CHEESE DIP
100g/3½ oz goat's cheese log
100g/3½ oz fromage frais,
  a little milk or soured cream

FOR THE FRESH HERB DIP
300ml/½ pint soured cream
3–4 tbls chopped fresh herbs:
  chives, marjoram, chervil, for
  instance, as available
salt and freshly ground black
  pepper

Either whizz the Roquefort and fromage frais to a cream in a food processor, or crumble the Roquefort into a bowl then with a fork, gradually adding the fromage frais until the mixture is smooth and creamy.

Make the goat's cheese dip in the same way; a food processor is probably best if the goat's cheese has a rind on it; or you could cut this off, depending on its state. If the dip seems a little dry when the ingredients have been mixed together, add a little milk or a little of the soured cream that you've got for the next dip, to soften it.

To make the fresh herb dip, put the soured cream into a bowl then stir in the chopped fresh herbs and some salt and freshly ground black pepper to taste.

Celeriac Terrine with Red Pepper Sauce

This is an excellent terrine which slices well either hot or cold and goes well with many autumn or winter vegetables.

700g/1½ lb celeriac
25g/1 oz butter
125g/4 oz Cheddar cheese, grated
25g/1 oz freshly grated Parmesan cheese
4 tbls snipped chives
3 eggs
salt and freshly ground black pepper
cherry tomatoes and chives to garnish

FOR THE RED PEPPER SAUCE
2 tbls olive oil
2 onions, peeled and sliced
2 red peppers
150ml/¼ pint stock
salt and freshly ground black pepper
15g/½ oz cold butter

Set the oven to 160°C/325°F/Gas Mark 3.

Line a 450g/1lb loaf tin with a piece of non-stick paper to cover the base and extend up the short sides; grease the other sides. Peel the celeriac, cut it into even-sized chunks and cook in boiling water to cover for about 15 minutes, or until the celeriac is tender. Drain – the water makes wonderful stock – then add the butter and mash, but don't purée because some texture is good in this dish. Mix in the Cheddar and Parmesan cheeses, the chives, eggs and salt and pepper to taste.

Spoon the mixture into the prepared tin and level the top. Bake for about 50 minutes, or until the terrine feels firm to the touch, looks golden brown and a skewer inserted into the middle comes out clean.

While the terrine is baking, make the red pepper sauce. Heat the oil in a saucepan, put in the onions and cook with a lid on the pan for 5 minutes. Meanwhile, wash the peppers and cut them into rough pieces – there's no need to remove the seeds because the sauce will be strained. Add the peppers to the onions, cover the pan again and cook gently for a further 5 minutes. Pour in the stock, cover and simmer for about 10 minutes, or until the peppers are tender. Liquidize the sauce, strain it into a saucepan and season to taste.

When the terrine is cooked, remove from the oven and slip a knife around the sides to loosen, then turn it out on to a warmed plate. Garnish with halved cherry tomatoes and small strips of chives. Just before serving, bring the sauce to the boil, remove from the heat and whisk in the butter, a little at a time, to make the sauce glossy. Serve with the terrine.

Other root vegetables such as carrots or parsnips could be used to make the terrine as a change from celeriac.

Warm Red Cabbage and Cherry Tomato Salad

Halfway between a cooked vegetable dish and a salad, this goes well with many winter dishes.

450g/1 lb red cabbage
1 onion
2 tbls olive oil
2 tbls red wine vinegar
225–350g/8–12 oz cherry
   tomatoes, halved

4 tbls snipped chives
salt and freshly ground black
   pepper

Wash and shred the cabbage as finely as you can; peel and slice the onion. Heat the oil in a large saucepan and put in the cabbage and onion, cover and cook gently for about 10 minutes, or until the cabbage is tender, stirring from time to time; finally, add the vinegar. This can be done in advance.

Just before you want to serve the salad, gently re-heat the cabbage; stir in the cherry tomatoes and chives, check the seasoning and serve.

Broccoli and Brie Bake

Although the flavour and texture of real Parmesan cheese cut from a block is best for many dishes, for this particular one, I prefer to use ready-grated Parmesan cheese from a carton. It makes a particularly dry, crunchy, golden-brown topping which contrasts well with the creamy sauce formed by the Brie melting into the cream in this dish.

700g/1½ lb broccoli
350g/12 oz Brie
150ml/5 fl oz single cream

75g/3 oz ready-grated
Parmesan cheese

Set the oven to 200°C/400°F/Gas Mark 6.

Wash the broccoli and cut the florets into smallish pieces. Pare the stems with a sharp knife or potato peeler to remove the tough, outer layer, then cut the stems, too, into small pieces. Cook the broccoli in 2.5cm/1 inch of boiling water, or in a steamer, for 4–5 minutes or a bit longer, until it is just tender. Put the stems in first and give them a minute or two before adding the florets which cook more quickly. Drain the broccoli and put it into a shallow casserole dish.

Cut up the Brie, including the rind, and add to the casserole, distributing evenly. Pour over the cream. Mash the broccoli and Brie into the cream a little with a fork, then sprinkle the Parmesan on top, cover it evenly. Bake for 15–20 minutes, or until bubbly, golden-brown and crisp.

Little Gem and Watercress Salad

Three little gem lettuces and a bunch or packet of watercress will be ample for this buffet. Have the lettuce and watercress washed and ready, stored in a polythene bag in the fridge. Make up a vinaigrette by putting 3 tablespoons olive oil into a jar with 1 tablespoon red wine vinegar, some salt and a grinding of pepper; shake well, then keep until required.

Just before you want to eat the salad, give the dressing a quick shake, then pour it into a salad bowl; tear the leaves roughly and put them in on top, toss the salad gently, and serve.

Compôte of Exotic Fruits

Lychees make a fragrant base for this, well worth the effort of removing their hard skins and stones. To these I've added pawpaws, which are sweet and excellent as long as they're ripe – they should be flecked with yellow and give a little when lightly pressed. Sharon fruits are ripe when they feel quite soft to the touch. Together, these fruits make a compôte which is sweet but refreshing and needs absolutely no accompaniment.

700g/1½ lb lychees   4 ripe sharon fruits
2 large ripe pawpaws

Remove the hard skin and stones from the lychees; put the flesh into a bowl. Cut the paw-paws in half, scoop out the shiny black seeds, remove the peel and cut the flesh into pieces. Add to the bowl. Quarter the sharon fruits, cut off the skin and slice the quarters into pieces; put into the bowl with the rest of the fruit. Give it a stir, then cover and leave for an hour or so, or until required.

The flavours will blend and the juices will run, making a little natural syrup; if you leave it overnight in the fridge, this syrup will become almost jellied.

Fruits Dipped in Chocolate

Choose a selection of fruits for this, according to taste; grapes, strawberries and physalis are particularly good. You can use all plain chocolate, or a mixture of plain and white.

225g/8 oz plain chocolate, at least 50% cocoa solids

about 700g/1½ lb assorted fruits

Break the chocolate into a bowl set over a pan of simmering water and heat gently until it has melted. Wash the fruits and dry them carefully, then dip them into the chocolate so that they are half-coated. Put them on a rack covered with non-stick paper and leave to set.

Chocolate Truffles

These are a bit fiddly to make, but they are a really special treat. This quantity makes about 30 truffles.

225g/8 oz plain chocolate, at least 50% cocoa solids, broken up
300ml/½ pint double cream

cocoa powder, icing sugar, finely chopped toasted hazelnuts to coat

Put the chocolate and cream into a bowl set over a saucepan of simmering water and heat gently until the chocolate has melted. Remove from the heat and cool quickly by placing the bowl in a bowl of cold water. Once it is cold and beginning to set, whisk it hard until it's thick and light – an electric whisk is best for this. (If it refuses to go thick, it isn't cold enough yet. Put the bowl back in cold water and leave for a few minutes longer.) Put the whipped chocolate mixture into the fridge to chill until it's solid enough to shape.

Sprinkle a tablespoonful of cocoa on to a plate, then, using two teaspoons, put generous teaspoonfuls of the chocolate mixture on top of the cocoa. Sift another tablespoonful of cocoa on top, dust your hands with more cocoa, then quickly roll the teaspoonfuls of mixture between your palms to make truffles, adding more cocoa to coat as necessary. Repeat the process using the other coatings in the same way. Put them on to a small plate and chill until needed.

Mulled Wine

Popular with almost everyone, mulled wine makes a very cheering drink with which to welcome your friends on a chilly winter's night.

2 oranges
12 cloves
1 cinnamon stick
2 bottles red wine

2 glasses Cointreau or other
    orange liqueur (about 50–
    100ml/2–4 fl oz)
a little sugar to taste

Scrub the oranges, stick the cloves into them, cut them into slices and put them into a stainless steel or enamel saucepan with the cinnamon stick, wine and liqueur. Heat gently to just below boiling point, then keep at this temperature for 10–15 minutes. Taste and add a little sugar as necessary. Ladle into warmed glasses and serve while still warm.

As an alternative to – or as well as – the mulled wine, I'd suggest serving a light dry white wine such as Muscadet.

INDEX

FOOD COMBINING INDEX

§

A Suitable for an alkaline meal in the Hay diet.
C Suitable for a carbohydrate meal in Michel Montignac's method but occasionally you may have to omit fat.
F Suitable as an all-fruit meal in Michel Montignac's method.
N Mix with proteins & starches in the Hay diet.
P Suitable as part of a protein meal for the Hay diet, or protein-lipidic meal in Michel Montignac's method but occasionally you may have to omit mustard, olives or nuts & substitute other vegetables for parsnips and carrots, and to sweeten with Canderel instead of sugar for Michel Montignac.
S Suitable for a starch meal in the Hay diet but occasionally you may have to omit lemon juice or vinegar.

GROUP A ITEMS
Autumn green salad with toasted hazelnuts 127
Baby brussels sprouts 171
Braised celery 115
Braised spring vegetables & herbs 16
Carrots in parsley butter 171
Christmas salad with truffle oil 172

Compôte of exotic fruits 178
Florida fruit cup 32
Frisée & orange salad 153
Golden peppers, stuffed 99
Lettuce & nasturtium flower salad 67
Little gem & watercress salad 178
Pink grapefruit, ruby oranges & mint 11
Ragôut of wild mushrooms 116
Roasted red peppers, stuffed 125
Roasted winter vegetables 151
Rocket salad 23
Spring fruit compôte 29
Spring fruit salad with violets 28
Sunshine ratatouille 59
Tagliatelle of summer vegetables 64
Tomato & basil vinaigrette 158
Vegetable goulash 152
Warm red cabbage & cherry tomato salad 176
Watercress cream 11
Watermelon & mint 51

GROUP C ITEMS
Chick-pea polenta with salsa 84
Golden roulade of lentils 149
Lemony rice 14
Lentils & coriander with yogurt sauce 103
Mexican beanfeast 132
Middle Eastern lentil soup 145
Pasta primavera 17

Purée of butter beans with rosemary & baked onions 155
Rich mushroom gravy 150
Spaghetti with spicy tomato & red pepper sauce 105
Spiced rice with leeks & red kidney beans 154
Spicy chick peas with yogurt & paprika sauce 104
Split pea & spinach dhal with raita & chutney 160
Summer bean & fresh herb salad 57
Summer spaghetti 62
Tomatoes, stuffed 66
Wholewheat pasta twists with broccoli & fromage frais 159

GROUP F ITEMS
Compôte of exotic fruits 178
Florida fruit cup 32
Jellied terrine of summer fruits 79
Pink grapefruit, ruby oranges & mint 11
Spring fruit compôte 29
Spring fruit salad with violets 28
Watermelon & mint 51

GROUP N ITEMS
Avocado salsa 134
Braised spring vegetables & herbs 16
Japanese-style salad with dipping sauce & gomasio 7
Nettle soup 10

GROUP P ITEMS
(*=Hay & **=Montignac)
*Apple & blackberry layer 118
*Apricot coulis 31
Artichoke bases, stuffed 110
Artichokes stuffed with lemon cream 55
Asparagus with hollandaise sauce 61
Aubergine, tomato & mozzarella bake 124
Autumn green salad with toasted hazelnuts 127

*Avocado salsa 134
Baby brussels sprouts 171
Bitterleaf salad with walnut dressing 102
*Blackberry fool 88
Braised celery 115
Braised spring vegetables & herbs 16
Broad bean pâté with grilled fennel 54
Broccoli & Brie bake 177
Broccoli & red pepper soup 147
Cabbage parcels with tomato sauce 107
Cabbage tagliatelle with cream cheese & mushroom sauce 157
*Carrots in parsley butter 171
Celeriac terrine with red pepper sauce 175
Chilled cucumber soup 56
**Chocolate mousse with orange cream 31
**Chocolate pecan brownies 136
**Chocolate truffle cake 73
**Chocolate truffles 179
Christmas salad with truffle oil 172
Christmas wreath 168
*Compôte of exotic fruits 178
Cream of celery soup 145
Cream of turnip soup 35
Cream of winter swede soup 148
Creamy tomato sauce 38
Curd cheese summer pudding 72
Curried root vegetables with coriander raita 156
Deep-fried Parmesan-coated Camembert with spring broccoli 18
Easy summer tomato soup 58
Egg salad mimosa 20
Fennel à la grecque 98
Fennel, tomato & black olive salad 62
Figs with mascarpone 121
*Florida fruit cup 32
French bean vinaigrette 79
Fresh herb dip 174
Fresh herb sauce 78

GROUP S ITEMS

Rose Elliot's Horoscope Service

Rose Elliot is a qualified astrologer as well as a cookery writer, and has many years' experience advising clients. Now she runs a computer assisted astrological service with her husband, which produces attractive reports describing the horoscope based on the actual time, date and place of birth. They can provide the following reports:

- **Personality Profile – PP**   **£15.00**
  This is a warm and sympathetic character portrait based on your birth chart, which describes the astrological reasons why you have the qualities and nature you have. It covers the basic temperament, emotions, health, energy, career, money interests and relationships. It has been very highly praised.

- **Children's Personality Profile – CP**   **£15.00**
  This profile covers most of the features described above but is written specially to help parents, and those bringing-up children, understand the child's needs, temperament, talents, energies, moods and preferences. It is especially appropriate for the 0 to 10 age group.

- **Future Trends – A 12 Month Forecast – FT**   **£14.75**
  The development of the birth chart reveals the experiences to be met year by year. Future Trends guides you through the next 12 months and shows the times of hard work and effort as well as those of success, fruition and joy; the times of stability and also those of change or transformation.

- **Comparison of Charts – CC**   **£19.00**
  This report compares two people's charts and shows their compatibility together. The attractions and the tensions; their ability to communicate and to have fun together. A first class guide for any couple in a relationship.

To order horoscopes please send the following details:

- First names and surname of client(s)
- Date, Time & Place of birth
- Sex of client(s): M/F
- Type of horoscope required (PP, CP, FT or CC)
- Name & Address for posting

Please enclose a Cheque or Postal Order for the full amount, or Credit Card details (Visa, Access or Mastercard, card number, name on card, expiry date).
Prices include Vat @ 17.5%. Vat Reg. No. 381 0276 67
Prices correct at time of going to press. If book is more than two years old please write for latest prices.

Rose Elliot Horoscopes
The Old Rectory, Church Road, Bishopstoke,
Eastleigh, Hampshire, SO50 6BH

Of further interest ...

Vegetarian Christmas

Festive Feasts for all the Family

Rose Elliot

Christmas is a time for celebration, a time for the family – and a time to eat.

New in paperback for the first time, Rose Elliot gathers together a whole host of imaginative and sumptuous recipes for the festive season, including party and buffet dishes, spectacular puddings, cakes and biscuits, and six superb Christmas day menus. Whether you choose cashew nut roast with herb filling or chestnut and red wine pâté en crôute, you will be creating food with a very special Christmas magic.

Each menu comes complete with tips, advice on freezing and planning ahead, and a specially constructed countdown to enable the cook to enjoy Christmas day as much as the rest of the family.

Not Just a Load of Old Lentils

The Ideal Introduction to Vegetarian Cooking

Rose Elliot

Rose Elliot's classic introduction to vegetarian cookery has been widely praised as one of the very best vegetarian whole-food cookery books ever written. From starters and salads to main meals, gateaux and desserts, she expands the basic vegetarian kitchen to include the colours and versatility of pulse-based meals using beans and lentils, savoury meat substitutes and a wealth of other vegetarian flavours. Special features include: a nutritional guide for vegetarians, a seasonal menu planner, recipes for slimmers, party themes and a clear glossary of foods.

Containing over 400 delicious recipes suitable for every occasion, this book is a joy to use and will delight all those who are familiar with Rose Elliot's enthusiastic and accessible style.

| VEGETARIAN CHRISTMAS | 0 7225 2852 3 | £7.99 | ☐ |
| NOT JUST A LOAD OF OLD | 0 7225 3037 4 | £5.99 | ☐ |

All these books are available from your local bookseller or can be ordered direct from the publishers.

To order direct just tick the titles you want and fill in the form below:

Name: _____

Address: _____

_____

_____ Postcode:_____

Send to: Thorsons Mail Order, Dept 3, HarperCollins*Publishers,* Westerhill Road, Bishopbriggs, Glasgow G64 2QT.
Please enclose a cheque or postal order or your authority to debit your Visa/Access account –

Credit card no: _____

Expiry date: _____

Signature: _____

– to the value of the cover price plus:
UK & BFPO: Add £1.00 for the first book and 25p for each additional book ordered.
Overseas orders including Eire: Please add £2.95 service charge. Books will be sent by surface mail but quotes for airmail despatches will be given on request.

24 HOUR TELEPHONE ORDERING SERVICE FOR ACCESS/VISA CARDHOLDERS – TEL: 0141 772 2281.